Cover Design: Dylan Grey
Interior Design: Janie Lee
Published by: 220 Publishing

Case #1988. Justin Ryan. First Edition.
ISBN: 978-1-5136-6368-5

TABLE OF CONTENTS

"Hello, and thank you all for tuning in. We have breaking news as we are reporting live from in front of J.R.M. Courthouse, awaiting the biggest case in history. Justin McMullen will stand in front of a judge just moments from now where his fate will be decided. Thousands are eagerly waiting outside for the arrival of the defendant. As anticipated, the crowds are divided on his innocence. While some believe that he has done nothing wrong, many believe that a guilty sentence is well deserved for crimes that have gone on for far too long. This is Your News Network, signing off—Wait! Is that him? Keep those cameras rolling, he just arrived!"

Today will be like no other. I'm on my way to stand in front of a judge who will send me to a prison that I had a hand in building. I knew this day was coming. The way life was headed, it was only a matter of time. The news crew surrounded me as I was taken out of the car.

"Mr. McMullen, why did you do this to yourself? Do you plan to seek help while in prison?"

"Justin, is it true that you are a danger to yourself? Are you suicidal?"

"There are reports that you have given up on life? Is this a cry for help?

I ignored the questions from the news crew. I walked down a pathway to the courthouse, accompanied by two police officers. On each side of the path were two crowds, bombarding me with their countless opinions.

"You're innocent! Keep Hope!"

"You deserve this! You did it to yourself!"

"Come on, Justin! Keep pushing! Don't give up!"

"No one wants you around! Why don't you crawl in the corner of your cell where you belong?"

The barrage of voices calling from the crowds was all too familiar to me. The divide amongst their viewpoints of me was reminiscent of my inner thoughts and how they clashed so consistently. I couldn't decide which side I agreed with anymore, now to the point that a judicial verdict had to be made. I was headed to a courtroom to lose the freedom that I felt I never obtained.

The courtroom was almost entirely dark inside. The only sources of light came from an open bulb above the Judge's seat and a spotlight hovering some feet directly over where I would stand. The two officers escorted me in front of the Judge. The contrasting shadows obscured his face, but his iconic, almost cliché black robe was clear enough to see. I couldn't provide a defense for this case, so I knew this sentence would come quickly. With all the evidence that they had on me, it was only a matter of time.

"Mr. McMullen," the judge said. "Please step forward."

"Yes, Your Honor," I said, taking a few steps toward him.

"Justin McMullen, the ruling finds you guilty of your crimes. You are sentenced to life in prison, effective immediately."

He took his gravel and hit the sound block.

Well...damn, I thought.

The two guards grabbed me by my arms and took me outside to the prisoner transport vehicle waiting out front along with the media waiting to spring the news.

"In one of the most historical trials of the decade, it all took a total of 5 minutes of deliberation before the jury had come to a definitive verdict on the McMullen trial. Now that the sentence had been officially made, Justin will now be escorted and excommunicated from the outside world as he immediately begins his life sentence."

I could overhear reporters buzzing with drama over the suddenness of the decision, drawing in the public's eyes and mouths more than they already had. Only the inside of the tinted squad car managed to quiet the cheers and protests.

A few seconds later, the truck finally maneuvered away from the crowds and the courthouse, taking me directly to my transport. After about a 20-minute drive, I was taken to a dock. A boat matching the tinted windows and all-black paint job of the truck I was in, was waiting to escort me to my destination proper. I was too caught up in my thoughts to retain much information when I was given the details of the prison itself. Still, the details that I managed to grasp onto were the facts of it being a single-cell prison, barred away from any interconnected land— an island prison.

As soon as I was shoved into the boat and locked away, I began my departure from everything I had ever known. No one would see me again. In a way, I felt a weight lifting from my shoulders. Yet, at the same time, perhaps because of that, the feeling of emptiness as well. In exchange for isolation, I was giving away the possibility of my life improving, aspects of which I had long since ignored.

I was given a green uniform to wear and a pair of brown high top boots. The removal of the tailored suit I wore for my trial was the final piece of normalcy I carried with me. With those gone, I officially surrendered my freedom. I was escorted to my cell, which only defining features were some chipped paint on the floor, a bed, and a small window.

What did I do to become a prisoner? I didn't hurt anyone. I didn't rob anyone. Internally, however, it was a different story. I'm not the only one who has been to one of these single-cell prisons. I'm sure that there are many more like me who are still in their cell right now. This is a story about one of those prisoners.

THE 1ST CHAPTER
Guilty until Proven Innocent

"Hey!" yelled a voice that bounced off of the walls of the cell. "You awake in there?

I opened my eyes, rubbing my hands through them, trying to get the sleep out. I looked toward the cell door to see one of the two correctional officers of the prison staring amused at me with a wide grin.

Nigel.

Nigel was wearing a blue police uniform and had a gold badge with the letter "N" on it covered in red. Nigel had strange looking gray crocodile-like skin, with slick black hair that he kept combed back. His teeth were pointed and sharp. So damn sharp, that it looked like he could bite the bars off of this cell if he tried. But his most defining feature was his red glowing eyes. Those things scared the hell out of me. They could burn a hole through anyone.

"I'm up now," I uttered.

"You overslept again. I should have woke you up earlier, but you know how my co-worker acts. By the way, I think you have more mail that came in today."

I shrugged as I sat up and removed my blanket from over me. Nigel's smile grew wider in response, showing off more of those razor-sharp teeth.

"Yeah, who needs em' anyway?" he said, leaning against the cell, "The less they know, the better."

"What's today?" I asked, stretching my arms above me.

"Does it matter?" Nigel chuckled, "It's the same as every day for you, kid. Not like you're getting out of here anytime soon."

I heard the gate at the end of the hall open, followed by loud footsteps. Someone was coming quickly toward my cell as if they were excited to see me.

"Hey, Justin," an upbeat voice said. "You're awake. How's the morning treating you?"

This officer was named Peter, who, like Nigel, I have known for all of my life. In every way, Peter was Nigel's opposite. His skin was transparent like glass, and it glowed with a strange white light. His pupil-less eyes glowed with the same light that the rest of his body had. Like Nigel, he wore a badge with the letter "P" on it and was covered in blue.

"The same as always," I said, placing my hands on the wall and kicking my leg back and forth to stretch.

"Well, I'm just happy that you are still with us. I have more mail for you that just came in. People who are trying—"

"I already informed him when he woke up," Nigel interrupted, " He declined once again. Those people don't mean him well, anyway. Come on, Peter, you know that."

"I don't know that," Peter said irked as he pushed Nigel away from the cell door. "In this situation, he needs to hear from the people that care about him."

Nigel chuckled and rubbed through his slick black hair.

"Ain't this guy the comedian?" he said, "You hear this, Justin? You're in prison, and this 'officer' wants you talking to the bad guys again. Are you stupid, Peter? The man already has to spend his life here, and you want him to take more punishment? You're brutal."

Peter reached in his pocket, pulling out envelopes. He extended his hand in the cell.

"Here," Peter said, "There are some people that want to talk to you. You could be missing out on something, Justin. You should at least take a look."

I sat back on my bed, almost frozen for a while. I put my head down.

"I don't want to read them," I replied, making a waving gesture for him to go away, "Toss 'em."

"Jay," Peter said, calling me by my nickname, "This is your family and friends we are talking about, man. What if someone is sick? Wouldn't—"

"I don't care!" I yelled. "Get rid of them. I don't want to see them."

Nigel snatched the letters out of Peter's hand.

"You heard the man," Nigel said. "Get them out of here. See ya tomorrow."

Peter sighed. He looked at Nigel and then slowly back at me.

"I'll be back the same time tomorrow to check on you, Justin," Peter said, walking off. "Hopefully, you're in a better frame of mind."

"He's in the right state of mind," Nigel barked. "The kid is starting to smarten up. Staying away from more trouble! This cell is the best thing that ever happened to him! He has peace of mind for once! You like tranquility, don't you, Peter?

I heard a metal door bang against the wall, letting me know that Peter had left, and I wouldn't see him for another twenty-four hours.

"I don't get that guy," Nigel said, opening the cell door.

For a brief second, I glanced at the opening in the cell door, but Nigel quickly noticed me.

"Don't get any ideas," he warned. "You know the dangers out there. You're safer in here. You know that. You couldn't leave this cell even if you wanted to."

I put my head in my lap. He was right, It was safer here than outside. There was nothing out there that the world could give me. If there was one thing that I could look forward to waking up each day, it was peace.

Nigel smiled as he went through the letters until he paused at one.

"Well, well, well. Look who we have here. It's a letter from your Mother. The first letter she has sent in a long time. Wonder what the hell this is about."

Nigel opened the envelope and unfolded the letter.

"Ahem," Nigel cleared his throat, "Hi son, just checking on you. I wanted to tell you that I love—"

"Nigel!" I yelled. "Just get rid of the damn letters."

That wicked smile showed itself on Nigels' face once more as he ripped up the letters and threw the pieces to the ground.

"Good call," Nigel said pleased, "You're learning. I would hate to see you buy into more lies. You're making the right decision by staying away from all that trouble. I mean, where did it ever get you? You lost money. You've been used and manipulated."

I nodded in agreement.

"It's the best move to make. This place is the only place for me now."

"You can say that again," Nigel said, laughing," You only got one life to live. What's the point of living miserably. Come on."

Listening to Nigel was hard to do at times, but it felt necessary. He seemed to be the most in tune with me. Whenever something crazy was happening, Nigel was nearly always the first to offer me advice. Peter would follow up with his own viewpoints to try and cool the fire within me. In the past, I would generally go to Peter when I needed to calm my mind, to which he would often fall back on old quotes like, "The past teaches us how to go about our future."

What was my past?

I was born in a small town called Champaign, Illinois, to John and Shirlean. I was the middle child of three boys. My older brother was named Cameron, and my little brother was named Jordan. We all grew up in the 90s and were relatively normal kids. My Father was a hard-working man that made sure that his kids had everything that they wanted. He gave me the nickname 'Jay' and was pretty much the sun in my sky. Dad was pretty exciting, as he always had a great joke to tell, and we shared similar hobbies. There were many days that I would sit and watch him play sports games like John Madden Football, which he would buy every year.

A series that he introduced me to which I still love to this day, was Street Fighter, a fighting-based video game series made by developer Capcom. As soon as he brought a copy of the game home for the Super Nintendo, my love for it grew and stayed with me for years. Due to his passion for video games, we always had the new gaming systems that came out. I don't think that there was a system that came out that we didn't have. Our collection of the latest video games rendered us the "cool kids on the block." Everyone knew who had the hot new games and where to play them. I remember on one summer day, we had almost every kid in the neighborhood at my house playing games. I honored my Dad. We were close for years.

My Mother was the moonlight in my sky. She was the caregiver of the family. Whenever there was an issue that required a particular amount of care, I would turn to her. There was once a time that I came home from school crying due to being teased. I ran back home as fast as I could and explained the situation to my Mother. She would always give me the comfort that I needed. One of the memories that I cherish the most is when I received the game The Legend of Zelda: Ocarina of Time as a Christmas gift when I was about eleven years old. My Mother and I were so fascinated by the world of the game that we would stay up, even on school nights, and play the game until 5am (my grades were terrific, so I was allowed to that year). Like my Father, I looked up to my Mother as someone to turn to at one point.

The relationship that I had with Cameron and Jordan was the stuff of legends. We would go on long bike rides, talk about all the cute girls, and do things that we weren't supposed to and laugh about it later. My older brother could draw, so I would sit and watch him work on our favorite cartoon characters. We both loved Street Fighter so much that I remember renting the animated movie one day from the video store. We must have watched it over fifty times, then go practice many of the moves we saw in our room. Jordan was the pretty boy of the trio; he was known for his hazel eyes and playfulness, which would get him into trouble. Cameron was our half-brother, and his Father lived in Indiana, so whenever Cameron would leave, Jordan was always there.

We grew up in a Christian home, where we learned about morals and lessons of what it meant to be responsible as young men. Our grandparents were a big part of that as they did all they could to make sure they set an excellent example for us.

Throughout the years, there were good and bad times that we had as a family. While we went through many changes, I was happy as a child until things got—

"Out of hand?" Nigel interrupted.

"I was just thinking—"

"Keep your head in the game. Those are nice thoughts in all but leave garbage where it is. Nothing good ever came from it. Look around you. I have to protect you from everything because of what happened."

I nodded and laid back into my bed and put my hands behind my head.

"Yeah, this is better," I said, " Maybe this is a blessing in disguise. Maybe, this is the way it is supposed to be."

The days turned into weeks, the weeks into months, the

months into years. Before I realized it, I spent over seven years in this prison. I listened to Nigel every single day. He consistently reminded me why I was in here, warning me of the dangers of the outside world. Peter would continue to try to get through to me. Still, his voice was getting softer, so much so that when he did come to visit, I was so entrenched in Nigel's words, that Peter's presence became nothing more than an irritation.

I became so used to this prison, that my cell became a sanctuary. It was just me and what seemed like everlasting dark peace. More letters came in from various people, but I still refused to read a single one.

There was just my cell. That's all I needed.

I Read Your File.

I woke up to three loud banging sounds that instantly knocked me out of my sleep. The sound of a nightstick ringing bluntly over the cell bars never failed to take me by surprise every morning. They were as familiar as an everyday alarm clock.

"About that time," Nigel said, "Rise and shine. Another day in paradise. How ya feeling?"

I rubbed my eyes and slowly sat up.

"I'm okay," I said, stretching my legs.

"You overslept again, but I'm sure it won't kill you," Nigel said, looking into the cell. "The mailman Peter hasn't shown up today. No letters, no false hope. Heh, he finally threw in the towel. "

I continued stretching, processing his information, while not properly responding to him just yet. The letters finally stopped. I didn't know how to feel about it. Apart of me wanted them to stop, but then there was another part that wanted them to keep coming. Someone cared enough to check on me and make sure that I was alright. It was a hypocritical thing to say, I know. As soon as I'd get those damn letters, all I'd do is get rid of them, burning any bridge that I had left. Jealousy would set in every once and a while learning of the "good news" of others. I stopped wanting to hear about who got married or some family trip that everyone went on. I got tired of hearing about what they were all doing or experiencing. It was a joke.

The metal door at the end of the hall opened while making a loud screeching noise.

"It's Peter. I did get another letter."

The sounds of footsteps once again were heading to my cell door; however, something sounded different. They were faster like Peter was running. Sure enough, he appeared in front of my cell, out of breath.

"Justin," Peter said, struggling to get the words out, "There is someone that is here to speak to you. A lawyer with interest in your case."

"A lawyer?" Nigel barked, "What part of 'life sentence' did you not understand? He's not—"

"—There is someone out there that says they can help you with your case. She has come a long way to speak to you. The least you can do is hear her out."

"She?" Nigel asked

I looked toward Peter, who had his whole arm in the cell with his hand open, reaching toward me.

"Come on. At least see what she has to say," Peter pleaded.

I stood as still as a statue staring at Peter. Nigel was standing next to him, shaking his head disgusted.

"You just keep setting this kid up to fail," Nigel said. "He already knows that there is nothing out there for him anymore. When are you going to get that through your head?"

"The better question is, how long is he going to pretend that he is safe in the cell that he's in?" Peter retorted.

Nigel let out a loud, amused laugh as Peter took out his keys, unlocked and opened the cell door as quickly as he could.

"You have got to be kidding me," Nigel barked, " Go ahead and talk to this lawyer. You are gonna come right back here, disappointed when the smoke clears. I guaran-damn-tee it."

"Why would a lawyer come now?" I inquired, "There's no way she could-"

"Exactly, no way anyone could or should drag him of this prison," Nigel barked with his fist clenched. "It's either this or the alternative, and we all know what the hell that means. Don't we?"

Peter, never taking his eyes off me while ignoring Nigel completely, walked up to me and put his hand on my shoulder.

"Give her your time this once," he said with giving a friendly grin, "What can it hurt?"

I took a deep breath and nodded in acceptance of his request.

Peter led me down the hallway, while Nigel watched amused.

"Remember, Justin," Nigel yelled. "Remember what we are trying to do here!"

I could hear Nigels' laugh as we walked away from the cell. The hallways Peter led me through would have been pitch black if it wasn't for the bulbs on the ceiling giving off a faint glow.

"We're almost there," Peter stated, "This lawyer seems legit."

"Let's hope," I groaned, preparing myself for disappointment.

"That sounded almost positive," Peter said as we reached the door. He turned the doorknob, and the door swung open. There was a silver table with two chairs waiting inside. Peter pulled out one of the chairs, then signaled me to sit down. I observed the room as I sat. Like the hallway, the bulbs on the ceiling gave off just enough light to make anything visible.

"She will be here in a few seconds," Peter confirmed, "I'll be right outside the door."

"Wait, what's her name?" I asked.

"Some fancy name, I believe," Peter said, closing the door, " Some fancy lawyer name."

Peter closed the door, leaving me in the room.

"God, what I'm I doing in here?" I said to myself. "What the hell was I thinking?"

Even though he wasn't in here, I knew Nigel would have said the same thing. As if he was right next to me, I could hear his voice speaking to me.

"Nothing will come of this. You know it won't."

"Come back to your cell."

"Get up! It's not safe out there!"

I stood up out of my seat, knocking the chair down to the ground and walked to the door.

"I can't do this," I groaned, " He's right. I—"

I then heard two knocks on the door. I quickly grabbed the chair that I knocked over and sat back down. The door opened with a woman in a blue blazer and shirt walking in. She was carrying a suitcase and had on blue high heel shoes. I was not able to see her face at all. From the neck up, there was this odd darkness around her face. I even tried to lean in and get a good look before she sat down. It was almost like the darkness in the room around her didn't want me to see her.

"Mr. McMullen," she said, "Good morning, how are you to-

21

day?"

Her voice gave off a motherly tone. It had a caring vibe too. It was intense but at the same time, gentle. As she sat down, I saw her brown-skinned hands open up a suitcase she placed on the table.

"Mr.McMullen?" she repeated, trying to get my attention. "Can you hear me? I asked how you are doing?"

"Oh," I said, snapping back to reality, "I'm fine. Thank you."

"Great, I thought that I had lost you for a moment," she said. "Good to see that you're still in the land of the living. Give me a second while I pull out your files."

She pulled out five brand new looking folders, all stuffed with papers inside. All the files had a title written in blue ink on them. They were numbered File #1 to File #5. They each had different colors: brown, yellow, blue, red, and black. Once she was done, she sat up in her chair and extended her hand to me, attempting a handshake, which I accepted.

"It's good to meet you, Mr. McMullen, finally," she said, " I was hoping that you would accept my invitation. I have read over your case, and I'm very confident that I can have your sentence overturned. With your cooperation, that is."

"What? Wa-wait," I said, confused, "I'm sorry, ma'am, what was your name again? I didn't get your name."

"Oh, it's some fancy name, "she proclaimed, "You wouldn't be able to say it right now, so for now, Ms. Lawyer will do."

"Ms. Lawyer?" I asked, dumbfounded by her odd suggestion, "That's what you want me to call you? Ms. Lawyer?"

"Effortless, right?" she asked, and if I could see her face, I was sure that she was sarcastically smiling when she said that.

"It's your choice," I said.

"Indeed it is," she professed, "So let's talk about yours: I was looking over your case. I see quite a few bits of evidence that I can use to get you out of here."

"How?" I doubted, "Didn't you hear about the sentence? The entire case lasted like 30 seconds. They had the verdict already decided for me before I even walked in the courtroom."

"Yes. I'm aware of that. You also didn't fight the case. Was there any defense ready?"

"I didn't have a defense. I'm sure you know that."

"Hmm...okay. Well, we are going to change that now," she reassured.

"We can try. I don't expect that we will make it very far."

"That was a half positive statement, which is good enough for me. Try, we shall, sir."

She opened up the brown file titled "File #1."

"Let's begin," she said, " I know a lot about your background already. You're Justin McMullen, born in Champaign, Illinois, yadda yadda yadda. Oh here we go, this is what I'm looking for. You are incarcerated for 'Self-inflicted-crimes.' They determined that you are a danger to yourself, which is the part of the case that I found very intriguing."

"Tell me about it," I said.

"It is also my understanding that you helped build this very prison. One cell, two guards with a hell of a lot of personal-ity, and for some reason, it's very dim. Visibility clearly wasn't planned very well."

"Can we just get to the point?" I said, slouching in my seat.

"Shall we?" Ms. Lawyer replied, "I want to go over these self-inflicted crimes. If we can get to the sources of the problem, we can make an excellent case for your innocence. Let's start with the root of this issue as it was the first crime charged against you. This crime took place when you were in middle school, Franklin Middle School, in 2002, to be exact. You went through some events that changed some of your personality, did it not?"

"Wow, here we go," I said already getting irritated, "Why even bring that shit—"

"Mr. McMullen," Ms. Lawyer quickly interjected, "Because you are my client, it is my job to have all the tools that I can use to win this case. So I wouldn't bring this 'shit' up without purpose."

"What purpose?" I asked.

"To win. And to do that, sir, I need to understand why you allowed yourself to submit to such a fate. I have studied these files extensively. If my theories are correct, I should be able to help you, but I need you to open up to me. Now, please. Tell me what happened to you. Any details, no matter how small, will be of great help to us."

"Fine. All right," I said, chuckling as I crossed my arms. "I'll play along. "

"Thank you. That makes my job easier," Ms. Lawyer said, taking out a pen and notebook. "Let's start with how you got to Franklin and then your experience so we can pinpoint this behavior.

File #1
Run as Fast as You Can.

One month before my last day in 5th grade, I learned that all of my friends would be going to a middle school called Franklin. As a twelve-year-old, I wanted to be a part of the crowd, so I told them that I would be going to Franklin. There was no way that I want to miss out on this school that I had heard so much about. I told my parents that I wanted to go to Franklin because all my friends were going there. I may have exaggerated some of the stories that my classmates had told me, but it was all just to get in. My Dad's co-worker, named Lee, informed him that he had a son who was going to that school, Desmond, who I met at the beginning of that summer. After meeting, Desmond and I quickly developed a great relationship. His family mirrored mine. He had two brothers like I did named LV and Lee jr. I would spend the weekends at his house when I could, and on Sundays, I would attend his church. While Desmond and I shared many personality traits, some clear differences became more apparent as time went by.

Desmond had an urban flair that I didn't have. He loved rap music, knowing more about the world of Hip-Hop than I did. I knew nothing about that genre. When he tried to explain a particular subject to me, I would look at him and pretend I understood what he was talking about. I grew up in a Christian household; my Dad was a pastor and had his ministry. Certain principles come with living in a religious house. I had heard some rap here and there, but I didn't pay much attention to it because we only played gospel music in our home. The only other genre that I listened to was house music, and that was because my uncle played in all the time.

Desmond loved rap, and I could tell that he knew about the history of it. At the time, I didn't realize how our differences would affect both the outlooks of our new school.

That summer, Franklin had a summer school program for 6th graders to give them an understanding of how the middle school system worked. It would last one week before the start of the school year. My parents took me to sign up for the program, with the trip being my first look at the school itself. The area that it was in was unlike any that I had been in before. It had a "hood" feeling to it. Once we arrived at Franklin, the staff gave us a tour of the building. It was much larger than any school that I had attended previously. Each section was for a specific grade level, with 6th graders being on the first floor next to the gym. I had a chance to take a look at the locker rooms where students received a lock for their gym clothes.

Once the tour and sign-ups were over, I went home excited to attend. The summer school program would start the following week. My Mother would drive me to Desmond's house so that I could catch a ride with his family since she had to go to work an hour earlier that day. His Mother drove us to Franklin, and we arrived five minutes before the start of class. Once I walked into class for the first time, it dawned on me that all the students were African American. I had lived in a mixed neighborhood, but for 11 years, we were the only black family on the block. All the schools that I went to while having some black students were, for the most part, predominantly white. As I walked to my seat, I heard a student say to me, "You dress like a white boy." The whole class erupted in laughter. I stood there, frozen in embarrassment. I had never really paid much attention to what I wore. They were just clothes. I sat next to Desmond and gave him the expression that asked, "What the hell was that about?"

Throughout most of the program, I stayed around Desmond as much as I could. I let him do most of the talking because he had a better grasp of how to relate to our new classmates. They used slang that I hadn't heard, so I felt left out when specific conversations were brought up. On the third day of summer school, I walked into the class with Desmond. For some reason, all of the students in the room were staring at me. I sat down in the back of the course, where one of the students named Wyatt told Desmond to come to sit with them for a second. The other students were laughing as Desmond stared at them stone-faced. When he walked back over to me and sat, I asked him what was up. He told me that they were laughing at me because I wore the same clothes for three days in a row. I didn't know how to respond because I didn't have much to wear.

After the last day of summer school, I walked out with Desmond, where I witnessed a brutal fight between two students. They starting fighting over something that one student said about the other. The confrontation ended with one student getting stomped into the ground.

"This year is going to be crazy," I told Desmond, but at that moment, what I was about to experience caught me so off guard, it would follow me for years.

That weekend, my parents went out to buy my school supplies and clothes. My Mother bought what she thought was acceptable for us to wear for the school year. I didn't have a problem with it at the time, because she bought what I liked. I thought that I was going to go into school looking amazing. I had so many plans for that year. I was going to make excellent grades, and I wanted to be on the honor roll once again. When the first day of the school year came, I put on my best outfit and went to the bus stop. She told me how cute I looked and that she was proud that I had made it to middle school. When we arrived at Franklin, I was about fifteen minutes late. I waved my Mother goodbye and went into the building. Everything went well for the first week: I met my new classmates, and I got used to the school system pretty fast, memorizing all of the class locations. I was catching the bus while being introduced to people that I didn't even know lived near me. Things were looking up.

Week two, however...was a little different.

As I walked down the hallway, there were a few girls that I knew from the bus I took to get home. I said hello to them, only for all there of them to flat out tell me that I was so ugly. They told me that they liked Desmond better, and he looked way better than me. I didn't know where that came from. I was dumbfounded while they laughed and walked away. When I got on the bus, they continued to talk about me the entire way home. This continued week after week. I would go back home in tears, heading to my room as soon as I got in the house. I tried to talk to my Dad about my new troubles. He would tell me "who cares what they think," stating he only cared about my progress as a student. My Mother would try to help me, but the fact that this would happen every day dealt a considerable blow to my personality, my identity. I couldn't relate to anyone at the school.

I was teased about the features of my appearance that I didn't even know that I had. I had a widow's peak in the front of my head, which was new to me. I started paying more and more attention to it after a student told me that it "looked stupid as hell." The clothes that I wore weren't "right" enough for anyone. I had no confidence to talk to the girls at my school at all. They were in another league. They were all developing at the age where guys at school would take notice. Sooner or later, naturally, sex became a talking point whenever we'd get the chance. My classmates around me would say stuff like, "man, I would hit that," or "damn, she got a fat ass." I started to believe that if I could get one of the best looking girls, I could prove something to everyone, even though at that time, I just wanted to prove something to myself.

My mind became detached from school due to this. I hated myself. Many of my interests were not considered cool. I liked Dragon Ball and Yu-Gi-Oh, which were deemed to be nerdy and lame. No girl I knew would want to talk about how my favorite anime characters from shows after school were dueling for their life and the fate of the world.

Most of the girls flocked around Desmond, always telling him how cute he was. No one ever said that to me. To gain that sort of notoriety, I adapted to my environment, even if it meant I had to pretend to be someone I wasn't. My grades were horrible. It should go without saying my parents were extremely displeased with me because of this. I can't tell you how many times I came home with my parents ready to whoop my ass due to how bad I was doing. It didn't matter to me at that point. I just wanted to be seen.

This new mindset of mine would be the beginning of an issue that I would carry for the next six years: the need for validation. So to do that, I started to imitate my classmates. I started using more profanity. I talked back to the teachers. I tried everything I could to get people to respect me more to show that I was just as cool as everyone else.

During the fall of that year, my teacher announced that there would be a school field trip coming up. All of the 6th graders would be going on a weeklong trip where we would be camping. I was excited about going because a girl I took notice of would be there. I was teamed up with about six other boys in one room. There were bunk beds, so we all chose one and talked during the nights. As the days went by, I was determined to get the girl that I liked to notice me.

On the fifth night, I approached her as she was sitting alone, working on a puzzle. We started a conversation that seemed to be going well enough. When I got her to laugh, she awarded me with her name, which was Stephanie. She had long black hair that I was crazy about, plus she had a beautiful figure. So mustering up all the courage that I had in me, I asked her out.

"Hell no. There are much better options," Stephanie said.

Again the blunt rejection left me feeling out of place. "My ambition, effort, and courage, stomped out on the spot, by the one girl I really wanted to get to know. I would rarely try to talk to another girl after that in fear that I was going to be told that they could do better than me, again. That school year changed the way that I viewed myself as a person. I allowed fear to settle in. I didn't want to go to the lunchroom with the other students anymore. Instead, I would hide in the bathrooms on the opposite side of the cafeteria's building. If I couldn't face my problems, I would try my best to stay away from them.

With that being said, the first year of middle school was pretty much a disaster, but it paled in comparison to the challenge that was the 7th grade school year.

Growing up in the '80s, my Father had a deep love for the love of basketball. We lived in a "Michael Jordan household," where we watched every one of his games. Watching my Dad get so excited while watching Michael inspired me to get into basketball, so I played whenever possible. I found myself loving the game in no time. There was a fire that burned within me whenever I played against another team.

My parents would sign me up to play in different programs to get me competitive. I hated losing. I wanted to get better every time that I stepped on the court as Michael did. Nothing ever seemed to get to him because he played with such a burning passion for the game, so I did as well. I went to basketball camps. I trained early in the morning and then got home to ask Dad how the game was supposed to be played. Dad had all of Michaels' NBA Finals appearances on videotape. I used them as a reference as I practiced. Every move that he made, I tried to mimic. I would have my little brother guard me so that I could practice Michaels' signature fadeaway shot.

With 7th grade year right around the corner, the only thing on my mind was making the basketball team. Making the team meant that I had to keep my grades up. I needed to be a full time student, which meant I needed to care about my progress in school. To prepare, I went back to summer school to be sharp by the time the school year started. I also went to another basketball camp to work on my jump shot. I wanted to be an accurate shooter, so I had my parents sign me up for a program specializing in shooting techniques. A cousin of mine named Verdell had also started a camp called Ft. Sooy and invited me to train. What made this camp different from others was that he taught the fundamentals of basketball and reinforced the importance of being a responsible young man.

Many of his lessons went in one ear and out the other. The only thing I cared about was proving to those at the school that I could make the team. I knew I was better than them. I knew in my heart that one of those spots on the squad was mine.

After the first three months of middle school, the day of tryouts finally came. The coach of both the 7th and 8th-grade team was named Todd, who we called Coach Anderson. It was going to be a three-day process where our skills would be tested. There were about forty students that showed up for tryouts. I stayed focus, putting everything that I had learned from the camps to the test. The first day went well. I showed that I had excellent ball-handling skills along with a solid stroke on my jump shot. Coach Anderson was tough on us and pushed us to our limits. I focused on his voice when he screamed:

"How bad do you want it?!?""

33

Each time he would yell this, no matter how tired I was, I forced myself to push past fatigue. Once the final day was completed, I knew that I left everything that I had on the court.

The following morning, I was the first student at the school that day. I ran up the stairs waiting for the list of players that made the team to be posted on the front door. There was a blue sheet of paper that had a list of names who made both teams on the front entrance. When I saw my name "Justin McMullen" on the list, I yelled so hard that the staff inside the building thought something was wrong. I called my Mother and told her the good news. When the rest of the students came to school that day, my new teammates walked up to congratulate me. We all hung out at lunch and after school playing basketball until practice. We formed a sort of brotherhood quickly. On the first day of practice, I played the best basketball that I ever had. Coach told us to be the best team in the state, we had to learn to respect the game. I felt the same way. Basketball had given me a lot to look forward to. I wanted to be one of the go-to players on our team.

When the first game we were scheduled to play arrived, I couldn't explain how excited I was. We were playing an away game in front of a big crowd. We were killing the opposing team. Coach Anderson put me in the game in the third quarter to see what I could do in a real game situation. It was the moment that I had waited for so long. All of the training that I had done led to this one point in time.

But, something was off.

When I got on the court, my body began to shake. I had

completely lost control of myself. Every muscle was so tight, and I didn't play up to the best of my abilities. After the game was over, I thought that I was just a little nervous. Then the second game happened, then the third game; it was the same feeling. Whenever I got on the court, I became so scared that I didn't even want to be there anymore. Why was I so frightened, though? I had always played in front of people, and not once did it throw me off. I played well no matter who was watching. Now, whenever I touched the ball, it felt like I was carrying a block of ice. It wasn't the same feeling when I was practicing. I was so shaken by the moment, I would do stupid things like throwing the ball out of bounds on accident. Not a single thing I did in camp ever showed itself on the floor.

It took me ten years to figure out why I had played so badly until, one day, it finally hit me. Everything I experienced about my time at Franklin before making the team made me unsure of myself. Basketball was the last place where I thought I would lose confidence, but it showed in my play. I didn't want to be anywhere near a court.

Basketball had started to betray me as it became just another source of embarrassment and anger.

The more time I spent on the team, the more I wanted off of it. I told my parents that I was quitting one day after a game. My Father said to me that if I left the team, that I would be in trouble. I didn't care, though; I just wanted to be free of getting laughed at. My coach told me that I would still receive playing time no matter what. He wanted me to ride out the rest of the season with my teammates to finish what I started. We got 4th in the state championships. While the team was saddened that we didn't win state, I couldn't have been happier that it was coming to an end. I didn't have to worry about making any more mistakes. I could try to forget about it all and try to get ready for the next year.

The following summer, I went back to basketball camp and started to train once again. I improved a great deal that summer, but the failures of the basketball team stayed with me. There was always this voice telling me:

"You are going to fail again."

"I'm going to make my family look bad."

"I'm going to make a fool of myself."

Nothing that I did would change what I felt could happen on the court. Coach Anderson became an instructor at the Ft. Sooy basketball camp that summer. He told me that I looked a hell of a lot better and couldn't wait to get me back on the team. The love of the game I once had, though, was no longer there.

I, for one, knew that I was not returning to Franklin.

I had enough. I thought that it was a mistake going to school in the first place. I was not like the other kids. They knew stuff that I didn't. I couldn't compare to my best friend, Desmond. Basketball, a game that I loved to death, scared the living hell out of me. So, my Mother gave me a choice: I could try one more time at Franklin, make the team and try to redeem myself, or I could attend a school closer to home called Jefferson. My Mother took me to Franklin once more for school sign-ups. My principal from elementary was going to be there, becoming the new principal for Franklin, and she begged me to come back. I told her that I was sorry, but I couldn't find it within me to return. I went to Jefferson with my younger brother, who was going into his first year of middle school.

For some reason, I attended all of the Jefferson vs. Franklin basketball games. I spoke to my old teammates, telling them that I was cheering for them. They told me that they would rather have me on the court with them. I asked them why, because all I did was embarrass the team. They told me that it didn't matter because I was like a brother to them. When I would go to their games, I would go into their locker room to visit. They never quit or stopped playing when they were losing.

That year, Franklin would win the state championship. I saw them on the news on the night that they won and I remember screaming at the top of my lungs. I saw my coach crying and my team all hugging one another. I stood there with a big smile on my face as I watched. But also tearfully.

I often wonder to this day to this day what would have happened if I stayed on the team. Why didn't I stay? Why did I run? For a while, I just thought that I was a weak person, too scared of a stage where people could see me. I had gotten better over the summer. I had the skills to compete. I could have done much good for the team, but it wasn't worth the pain of failure in my mind. It was not worth going home in tears over every mistake that I had made. I couldn't deal with it any longer, even if it meant not playing for the team.

Then one day, I just quit basketball. I don't even remember stopping, it just happened. I ran away from the game I loved all my life to that point.

Soon running became the answer for everything.

Protection.

"Thank you, Mr. McMullen," Ms. Lawyer said, closing the file. "That was a great help in understanding the situation."

"Wait, that's all you needed?" I asked, confused, "What about the other four files?

"Baby steps, Mr. McMullen, baby steps," Ms. Lawyer said, putting the files into her suitcase. "I'm so glad that you were willing to see me. It seems that you have lost a lot of confidence in yourself, and that came with much-misguided thinking. Wanting to be accepted by others is in human nature, but it looks like this problem stayed with you for some time. Once I review the information you have given me, we will pick this up tomorrow morning."

She stood up, adjusted her skirt, grabbed her suitcase, and walked toward the door. She turned my direction though I still couldn't see her face.

"See you tomorrow, sir," she said.

I heard Ms. Lawyer and Peter talking for a moment, then clacking of high heels faded as Ms. Lawyer walked away. The door opened once again, with Peter standing in the doorway. He helped me out of my seat and walked me back to my cell.

"How did it go?" Peter asked.

"I'm not sure. Seemed like she was gathering information." I said, " But how did she find out about the case again?

"She told me that she has been looking into it for some time. Seeing how long you guys were in there, she wasn't kiddin'."

Peter walked me back to my cell once again. There was complete silence on the way back. When we arrived at the cell, I walked in and sat on the edge of the bed. Peter closed the cell door and stood there for a moment.

"What is it?" I asked him, "Gonna give me some more kind words?"

"I don't mean to pry," Peter said, "but I heard what you two were discussing. That year was something, wasn't it?"

"You were there," I said, "You saw all of it."

"Things happen, Justin. You made the team. Don't you remember how many people said that you didn't have a chance that year? Your classmates were trying to fight you at recess just because your name was on the team list."

I chuckled as the memory hit me.

"Yeah, yeah, I remember that. One of my classmates named Johnathan, walked up to me and asked, 'how did your trash ass make the team over me?' I just smiled at him. That was a good day. I can't front about that."

"You had a lot to be proud of that day. You were the first person on the team to see the list. It was kinda funny watching you work at the tryouts. Your eyes were wide the whole time."

I laid down on my back on the bed and stared at the ceiling.

"I wanted it, man. I needed to be on the court that year," I said, rubbing my face. "But I guess the court had other plans, didn't it?"

"You deserved to be there. You were a little shook, but you deserved the spot on the team. Deep down, I believe you know that."

"Do I?" I asked, annoyed, "There were few games where I

didn't make a mistake. I have no idea how Coach didn't kick me off the team that year."

"Maybe you didn't get kicked off the team because there was a belief that no matter what you did or how scared you were, your coach knew he made the right decision. I know looking back at it for what it was, it didn't seem that way. But you were the right man for the job."

"You know that I don't believe none of that, right? You saw what happened, so you telling me that bullshit over and over ain't really helping," I said. "Is there anything else? I'm in my cell now, Officer."

Peter pressed out a sigh as he locked the cell door.

"The lawyer will be back in the morning to continue discussing your case with you. I suggest you try to get a decent rest for once. Nigel will be on night duty again."

As he turned away, I caught him shaking his head to himself. Peter quietly began to amble down the hallway.

"See you in the morning," he said.

I turned to my side, where I was facing the wall. I never thought that I would have to reminisce about Franklin again, but what caught me off guard was the fact that it stayed with me for so long. Reminiscing about what happened at Franklin was like reliving it all over again. I don't think I even expressed to my parents or Coach how much it bothered me at the time.

"I'm very confident that I can have your case overturned."

I kept repeating what "Ms. Lawyer" kept saying over and over again in my head. Even if I did make it out of here, what the hell was I gonna do? I don't have any goals or motivations to

speak of. That well dried up about a year before I got in here...
but maybe some of what she said made some sense.

"Trying to go back to La-La land, huh?" An unnerving tone
pierced the dead silence.

The voice almost made me jump out of my bed. I quickly
turned around to see two red eyes staring at me from outside
the cell.

"Nigel," I said, trembling. "I—"

"No need to explain," he said while opening the cell gate, "I
told you I hear everything. I'm just here for night duty."

Nigel slowly opened the cell door and began to approach
me. His demeanor was noticeably different than usual. The
way he strolled in, it was like he was closing in on his prey as he
grinned.

"We are friends, right?" he asked, standing over me.

"Ye-yeah," I replied, slightly hesitating, "Of course we are."

"Then let me give you some 'best buddy' advice. You don't
want to go back to the same garbage that got you in here. This
lawyer who came to see you today told you that you could get
your case overturned, didn't she?"

"Nigel, look," I said, slowly scooting myself back on the bed
to put more distance between us. "She just said that she wanted
to look into the case. That's it, man."

Nigel's abnormal grin always filled me with vibes of someone who knew how to turn a situation in his favor. If faced with a
problem or scenario, a straight-forward approach would always
land him on top. But this face glaring at me wasn't the Nigel I
had grown familiar with over the years. His toothy smile was po-

larizing. Something about the extra effort he put into his expression was vile. It wasn't so much of a person in control anymore. It was about exerting a sense of control.

Intimidation.

"Friends don't lie, Justin," Nigel said, his words seethed through his teeth "Do you remember all the warnings that I gave you? How many times did I save you from embarrassment? All of a sudden, some noisy bitch comes around, and you start getting ideas."

"It's not like that, man," I said, tensing my body up to stifle my shaking, "I'm just hearing her out."

There was a chilling moment of silence between us. Nigel's eyes never left mine. I didn't know what he was going to do next because he knew that I was lying. Somehow he always knew when I was. Then, out of nowhere, his barely masked sneer began to cool itself, settling back to his standard poker face grin.

"...This place is home now. Homes come with peace. We like our new peace, don't we, Justin?"

"Yeah," I quickly responded, "This is home."

"Good," Nigel said, walking out of the cell, closing it behind him. He took the keys and locked the door, then gave me one last glare. He put the keys to his cell on a chain attached to the belt on his waist.

"That's good."

He walked down the hall. I laid back on the bed, trying to regain my composure.

"Damnit," I said, rubbing my face. Even my eyelids were

twitching out of fear.

This lawyer that came out of nowhere, who was she? There was something more to her than the files she brought to our meeting. I had never met anyone like her before. These "baby steps" she was talking about. I still wanted to understand why she would take this case and why the hell she would do this for someone like me, who wanted to be in this cell.

THE 2ND CHAPTER
The Mountains You Can't Climb

"Rise and shine," said a voice. "Sorry about last night. I had to give you a little reminder of what we are trying to accomplish here."

I rolled over to my side, where I was once again face-to-face with Nigel glaring down at me. I barely slept last thinking about what happened the previous day.

"The lawyer is going to be here in about an hour. Peter will be here to escort you to her."

"Okay," I said, sitting up on the edge of the bed and massaging my side. "I'll be ready."

"Yeah, you will be, and you will remember what I told you last night. The lawyer chick? She's no good for you—no good for us. I've seen her type before. She'll try her hardest to pretend like she cares when all she is doing is leading you into more trouble. You're tired of trouble, aren't you?"

"I am," I sighed, "I don't want any more of it. I want to be happy. I want to be free like I always wanted."

"Good. I'm on your team. That's all I'm trying to get at. Today I want you to tell her that you don't want to see her anymore. There is no light out there in the world. Just a bunch of brain-dead asses doing anything that they can to get what they want. They don't give a damn about what they do or who they hurt. That's not you. You're different. Keep your eyes on the prize."

The Prize.

No one understood the prize that I was chasing. I wanted to resolve all my problems by getting away from my past life. I wanted to be someone better, someone stronger. There was no need for anyone else. It was as if they were always taking something from me and never putting it back.

But if that's the case, why did I feel the need to talk to Ms. Lawyer so bad?

Nigel walked out of the cell door and gave me a wink after closing it. Shortly after, I heard the door at the end of the hallway open once more.

"Justin," Peter called, approaching my cell to open the door, "It's time. The lawyer is already in the room waiting for you."

I stood up slowly, trying to ignore how tired I was.

"Are you, okay," Peter asked, "You look terrible. Did you get any rest at all last night?"

"Yeah, I'm fine. Rough night."

We walked down the hallway, heading to the interrogation room. Nigel hadn't gotten that aggressive in a long time. Sure he'd act like that on rare occasion, but I knew that he was doing what he felt was best for me. We arrived at the door, and Peter opened it. When I walked in, Ms. Lawyer was sitting at the table with a yellow file titled "File #2". The room was somewhat brighter than last time, but I still couldn't see her face.

"Mr. McMullen, you look well today," she said.

Peter pulled out a chair from under the table and gave me the signal to sit down. I slumped in the chair, holding my head up to force myself to stay awake.

"Okay, maybe you don't. What's the matter?"

"Long night. I must have slept the wrong way."

"You sure? Because from my point of view, it looks like you never shut your eyes last night even to blink ."

"No, really, it's fine. I'm ready to start now."

"Mr. McMullen, listen. If anything is going on, you should tell someone before it gets out of hand. With your current predicament, I would think that you would at least understand that."

"I said I'm okay! Let's just get this shit over with."

Ms. Lawyer let out a frustrated huff.

"Alright. How do you feel about our last meeting?" Ms. Lawyer asked while looking through the folder.

"Still trying to figure out the manner of our defense, I guess," I said.

"That will come in time. You'll just have to trust me for now. After reviewing the information you gave me yesterday, I realized that certain walls were placed within you that hindered your confidence. Do you agree?"

"You can say that," I said as I looked off to the side, leaning back into my chair.

"Do you believe that they played a part in why you are in here?"

"What do you mean?"

"Well, you're in this prison on the charges of 'Self-inflicted crimes,' Mr. McMullen. And walls take time to build. You could say what you experienced was the blueprint for this unfortunate ordeal."

"Huh? Up until now, I never looked at it that way. You get used to things going a certain way. It goes on for so long, and you lose sight of how you got there."

"Finally, a full answer for once. Now we are getting somewhere," Ms. Lawyer spoke while opening up the file. "That opens the door to file number two. I want to look into your relationship with your entire immediate family at some point. For now, I want to speak to you about the first two years of high school. I also have questions about your two brothers that you have, Cameron and Jordan."

"What about them?"

"I understand that you three were close as children. Sometime during high school, the bond you had with them got a little rocky. What do you believe was the cause of that?"

"I don't—"

I paused for a second, thinking about how to answer the question.

There were so many answers I could give. I hadn't spoken to either of my brothers for a while now. I felt disdain toward them. It was a bitterness that I carried every time they would come up.

"Is this one of your weapons for our defense?" I asked.

"Of course it is," Ms. Lawyer answered instantly, "Every bit of information helps."

"This one doesn't. You're going to have to use another angle."

"Mr. McMullen," Ms. Lawyer reached to her face, then placing her pair of glasses on the table. She leaned back in her seat, taking a moment to rub around the bridge of her nose. "I don't want to remind you of my job here, but I'm here to help you face this situation. And sometimes that's going to include bringing up pieces of your life that may be a little sensitive for you to touch on. So you're going to have to toughen up just a little bit for me, okay?"

I sighed, putting my head down to take a moment to myself, then nodded in agreement.

"Thank you. God, I don't get paid enough for this," 'Ms. Lawyer muttered beneath her breath, reaching back to her glasses. They faded back into the dark when she placed them back on her face.

"Moving on the subject at hand...tell me about your freshman and sophomore years of high school. I need you to be as detailed as possible. You have the floor."

I stood up out of my chair and leaned against the wall behind me. I took a deep, long breath.

File #2
Three Minus One.

2004 would be my first year of high school at Centennial. I was nervous because, for the first time, everyone I knew from both Franklin and Jefferson would be at one school. In my head, I wanted to do things differently. I heard that there was a school football team where anyone could join. I told my Mom about the opportunity, but she was more concerned about my grades. After a long talk, my parents told me that I could join as long as I put school first. Even though I told them I would put more effort into my education, I wanted to try out another sport. Basketball was not an option. I didn't even bother to look up when tryouts started. Football was exciting for me because my family enjoyed watching it at the time. My Mother dropped me off at one of the practices where multiple people I knew from both middle schools were already on the field. I walked up to the coach and asked if it was okay to join the team. He welcomed me with open arms.

While I wasn't the biggest physically on the field, speed seemed to be everything. I ran a 4.4 on a forty-yard dash, which was pretty good. My coach gave me the position of cornerback on the defensive team. We would practice four times a week. Our coaches made sure that I knew all of my defensive plays and schemes. The game was extremely technical. Every single position had a purpose on the team. If one part failed, the whole team would fall apart. It made the team that I was on feel more like a family, even more so than basketball did. There were plenty of times that I felt that football was the game for me. I loved it so much. I carried my mouthpiece with me everywhere I went. Once we received our uniforms, I would wear my helmet around the house all the time.

Learning more about the NFL's extended history became an interest of mine. I studied some of the great cornerbacks in football, hoping that I could learn from them. I got along great with my teammates also. Because I grew up with most of them, developing a relationship with them was easy. We would joke around and sing stupid songs in the locker room, which I would start. I became more open to expressing myself because I was having so much fun. I had a great relationship with my coaches, as they were as goofy as we all were, but they kept us in line. The summer training continued, and I felt myself getting physically stronger. If I made a mistake on the team, I made sure to apologize to my teammates. I tried to be the one on the squad that held us all together. I didn't allow us to fight with each other. We would talk about any issues we had and laugh about it later.

Soon, the time came for the big scrimmage on the varsity field. I was so excited to play that day, I don't think I did anything but watch football. When I got to school, I could hear the crowd roaring. The varsity team was on the field first. As I got my pads and uniforms on, I thought about how I would make the best of this situation. I could redeem myself. I put on my helmet and headed to the field. I knew I had one job: Hit anyone who had the ball. I never knew that I could run so fast while I was playing. I knew I was quick, but I didn't realize how fast my body would react to the action around me.

I remember one of my teammates named Taylor was running with the ball out of the end zone on a punt. I saw him and ran toward him as hard as I could while building up anger for a big hit. He tried to stiff-arm me, but I hit him away. Any other time before this, I wouldn't have thought I couldn't even take him down because he was so much bigger than I was. A few plays later, I did the same thing to my teammate named Derrick. He was running near the sidelines with the ball. I ran at him with all the energy that I had in my body and knocked him out of bounds. My team roared in support of my tackle. My Coach kept yelling, "There you go, McMullen!"

When the scrimmage was over, the coach told us who was going to start. I had made the second string on the team. I was a little bummed at first not being a starter, but I had come late to training during the summer, so I didn't mind it. I was going to work hard to move up soon when the time was right. I didn't even know who started above me, but it didn't matter. I'd have my chance someday.

In a blink of an eye, summer vacation was over. The first day of high school had come at last. High school was similar to middle school as far as classes went, only everything was twice as big. The gym was gigantic compared to what I used to. The cafeteria served foods that you would see in fast-food restaurants around town. The staff allowed us to go off campus to either return home or go out to the local restaurants for lunch. We had more responsibility. I would spend much of my time with my middle-school friends during the lunch period. As for interest in girls went, we were in the big leagues now. There were way more beautiful girls in school now. And every girl that I knew had changed in some way. Sex wasn't only circulating in the head of just guys anymore. The girls talked about it like they wanted it just as bad as we did. More so than just talking about it, they displayed it all the time. Their fashion changed as they dressed more mature than their middle school years. So freshman life seemed like it was going to be exciting. And for a while, it was.

Our first game as the freshman football team was on a sunny Saturday. The varsity team and junior squads had lost to some team from out of town. My freshman squad made it clear that we were not taking a loss in our first game. The other team that we were playing had on black jerseys and white helmets. I wanted to beat them badly because they reminded me of the Sharks, a team that I saw in the movie "Any Given Sunday." Kickoff came, and we scored the first touchdown of the game.

Strangely, Coach decided to put me in as a wide receiver, which I didn't know much about because I always practiced with the defensive teams. I was given the play, the huddle broke, and I lined up with the team. The quarterback hiked the ball, but a flag was thrown on the play. Because I had not lined up correctly, my team received a penalty. The coach took me out of the game. After that play, I never saw the field again that game. We had won easily though, with the score being 27-0. We celebrated in the locker room as we were the only team at our school that won their first game.

On the way home with my parents, I thought about the mistake that I made telling myself that I wouldn't make the same mistake twice. This situation was familiar to me, but I didn't want to reach back in the past, so I avoided thinking about it for too long. I trained as hard as I could in the practices after the first game to see some field time. The next match was against Danville, so I needed to be ready. On the team bus there, I was my cheerful self, but I wanted to be in the game with my teammates. Once we got there, we changed into our uniforms while the coach went over our strategy. The game began an hour later. I waited on the sidelines anxiously for my turn to get in.

I waited and waited.

Then the final horn had sounded. We had won 21-14. It was a comeback victory. After the game, I asked Coach why I didn't get in. He told me that the game was tight and we needed our best players there. I nodded in agreement even though I felt that I was a good player. I could have helped the team in some way. The ride home, I was entirely utterly silent. When my teammates told me to cheer up, I let them know that I wanted to be left alone. Once again, I tried to prove myself in practice. So I trained harder. I learned more about the playbook. I went over all my assignments.

Game after game passed. I received no playing time. My parents came to a couple of my games, but they never saw me play at all. Thoughts of Franklin started to creep in. It was the same experience all over again. I cheered for my teammates as I should, but I grew frustrated. One practice, I got into an argument with one of my coaches because I wasn't playing in games. He told me to run some laps around the field for back talking. During the lap, I got into it with one of my teammates for a joke that he made. Another teammate heard the argument and told me, "Who cares what you think? You ain't never getting any playing time anyway." As much as I wanted to cuss him out for what he said, I knew he was right. I had concluded that I wasn't going to play, no matter what I did.

I decided that if I didn't get any playing time before halftime on our next game, I would quit right then and there. While on the sidelines, I told a teammate what I was going to do. He begged me not to leave. He told me that I was one of his favorite teammates. He said that the team needed me, and soon the coaches would give me my shot. I explained to him that this has happened to me before and that I was tired of being overlooked. When halftime came, I made good on my promise. I ran to the locker room, changed clothes, and then headed home. I told my Mom that I had quit the team, saying that it was "just Franklin all over again."

In gym class the next day, my coach confronted me, asking me why I quit on the team. I yelled at him, telling him that the team had quit on me. I was breaking my neck during practice only to see other teammates were getting playing time. He told me that it was a shame that I quit because he enjoyed having me apart of the team. I was developing into a good player. He said that he would leave the door open for me if I ever wanted to rejoin.

I then told him, "It wasn't like you were going to let me play anyway."

I never returned to the team that year or played in any sports at all after that conversation.

With football now gone, I was just a full-time student. I would now turn my attention to the social totem pole of high school. It became quickly apparent that I had the same issues that I had in middle school. I didn't have any fashionable clothes. I would go as far as to say that I had about two pairs of pants, three shirts, and an old Michael Vick jersey that I had been wearing since the seventh grade. Like before, everyone somehow noticed this. My friends use to tell me that after that year, I had to get rid of that Vick jersey that I wore. Everyone talked about the way I dressed. For the life of me, I never knew why I received so much attention for that. There was a particular girl that always had an issue with me. In my biology class, she would contently make fun of me in class, mocking me in front of everyone. At first, I ignored it. I didn't want to go into a back and forth battle. The situation got worse because I never addressed it. She would spread rumors about me, which the whole school would know.

My crew that I hung with seemed to be having much better luck around the school. Many of the girls liked them; they were always hanging around and giving them compliments on how they looked. I was full-blown jealous of them. And they stayed on top of fashion statements at the time as well. They always had name brand clothes that I was dying to get my hands on. They had a way with the ladies and were able to speak to them with confidence. My self-esteem couldn't handle that yet. Whenever they were around girls, I acted as if I wasn't even there. My disdain for my friends grew to the point that I stopped hanging around them. I held a little hatred for them because of how much better they seemed than me. With my thoughts only on my social status in school, my grades plummeted.

My parents' frustration with my grades had hit a boiling point one night. My father rushed into my room, yelling at the top of his lungs. He told me that he was sick of me not ever trying in school. He said the only thing I ever focused on was what the people around me thought of me. He warned me that if my grades didn't improve, I would grow up to be a nobody working a dead-end job. He slammed the door, not wanting to hear anything that I had to say.

I had hit a new low that year. I didn't want to go to school at all. I waited outside until the first hour finished, so I wouldn't have to deal with getting embarrassed again. I would throw my report cards away so my parents wouldn't see my grades. I spent a great deal of time in the counseling office speaking to a counselor named Mrs. Marshall, with whom I developed a friendship. She would always tell me to focus on my grades and not to put so much thought into what someone said about me. She was sure that I could graduate if I put more effort into my education. Being young and dumb, though, I didn't take her advice. I didn't want to go through high school the same way I did in middle school being a nobody.

I met a junior named Katrina through a physical development class. We had talked one day, and she seemed to be really into me. She had short brown hair, with a beautiful curvy figure. Many of the other guys seemed to like her, so I was excited that she wanted to be around me. We hung out for months. We became great friends and talked about everything. Soon, I told her that I liked her. I wanted her to be my girlfriend, but she told me that I was too young. It drove me crazy when she said that because she always gave me the signs that she liked me but wouldn't be with me. Regardless, we stayed friends. At times we would talk about sex. She would explain to me how I should speak to women if I wanted them to date me. She told me that she would even consider dating me if I would stop acting so depressed at school all the time. Katrina was my first big high school crush. For a while, I thought that we really would be together at some point.

One night, before I went to the movies, I called her to see how she was doing. She told me that she was fine, but she had something to talk to me about. I was prepared to say to me that she wanted to date finally, but the news I was about to receive was the polar opposite. Katrina had a new boyfriend now. She apologized for leading me on, along with some other shit that I didn't want to hear. My heart sank. I hung up the phone and went to the movies with parents while trying to forget what she told me. On Monday of the next week, I saw Katrina in the hallway while I was walking to the bathroom. She gave me a soft smile and waved. I returned her hello with an angered look. I walked away from her without saying a word. We never spoke again after that.

I turned to video games as a form of escape. I stayed in my room on the weekends, skipping out of any school events. The number of friends that I had decreased. I wouldn't even entertain the idea of going out of the house if someone had invited me. I started to compare myself to everyone, even people that were on television. Unexpectedly, that jealousy would cause me to turn on the two people that I never thought that I would ever have any animosity toward.

I didn't speak to my brothers, Cameron and Jordan, about my problems much. I was on good terms with them, but I started to notice how much attention they got. One day, Jordan came to my first-hour class to pick up some lunch money. Every female in the damn classroom walked up to him and told him how cute he was. One of the girls that I liked told me that she thought my brother was more attractive than me. She followed up with that saying that she may have to get with my brother when he comes to high school. This got worse when my brother attended Centennial with me. He had no problem picking up the chicks that I liked.

He was known for his hazel eyes.

My eyes were too big.

He was attractive.

I was not.

It was the same situation with my older brother. I remember walking in a store with those two and my Mother one day. The store clerk told my Mother that my two brothers were gorgeous. She never looked my way a single time. In the car on the road back home, I told my Mother, "I might as well not even be your son." I turned my back to them after some time. I wanted nothing to do with them, and they had never done anything ever to make me feel that way. They were like mountains; no matter what I did, I could never climb over them. For the first two and a half years of high school, this anger built up inside me.

I wanted to be loved.

I wanted people to say complimentary things about me.

I wanted validation.

I'd often daydream that I was famous. I'd imagine what could happen if I had a nice car and a gorgeous girl in high school. That day never came. I felt that no matter what I did with my life, I'd always be overlooked.

Still Here.

"Why did you not talk to your brothers?" Ms. Lawyer asked, "Did they ever try to reach out to you?"

"They did a few times, " I replied. "But at that time, they weren't my brothers anymore. They were like everyone else that I was jealous of, ya know?... So are you going to tell me that it was stupid for me to feel that way?"

"No. No, I'm not," Ms. Lawyer softly replied. "With all that you had just told me, I could see why one would feel that way. Feeling overlooked and never appreciated can eat away at you. Can I ask you a question, though? I hesitated to ask this until now, but now that we have gone over the second file, I feel it warranted. Why do you feel that you need to go outside of yourself to be noticed?"

"What do you mean?" I asked, sitting back at the table.

"What was so wrong with being Justin?" Ms. Lawyer asked.

"No one seemed to notice," I said.

"...did you notice yourself?" Ms. Lawyer asked.

I sat back in my seat. I felt tears slowly begin to well up as her words sunk in, which I quickly wiped away, tightening my jaw as I bit my bottom lip.

"Nah. No, I didn't," I said. "Look, why the hell are you doing this? Really? There are a million things that you could be doing? Why the hell would you take this case?"

"Because there are some things in the world that are worth it, Mr. McMullen. Even if you think you're not one of them."

Ms. Lawyer put the file into her briefcase and placed it on

the floor. She then sat upright in her seat.

"So, what happened to your brothers?" Ms. Lawyer asked.

"Still around. And still crazy about me for some reason. I use to talk shit behind their backs. They never cared about that. They would just forget about it the next day. I remember Cameron telling me once that he thought I was 'acting like a bitch' at one point," I said, chuckling, "But he said that he knew that I was going through something. He never turned on me no matter what happened."

"It seems like you still have some allies left," Ms. Lawyer said, "Have they tried to reach out to you since you've been here?"

"They have sent me letters, but...I haven't read them."

"They still need you. Your family still needs you. When we win this case and walk out of here, you should go back to them and make up for the lost time." Ms. Lawyer said. "You may be missing out on something."

"They don't need me; trust me. We are better off without each other," I said, putting my head on the table.

"...Did Nigel tell you that?" Ms. Lawyer asked.

I raised my head, looking at her enraged.

"What the hell do you know about Nigel!? He was only trying to protect me this whole time. I'm safe, and you have no right or reason to judge me!"

She stood up, adjusting her uniform before picking up her files and briefcase, and promptly made her way to the door.

"We will pick this up tomorrow, Mr. McMullen," said Ms. Lawyer, reaching for the doorknob, "One more word of advice before I go, sir. The company that you keep is a reflection of yourself. I'll see you in the morning."

She walked up to the door, and knocked three times.

"Officer, we are finished for the day." Ms. Lawyer said.

"Okay, I'll have him ready to go tomorrow," Peter replied. "Justin, let's roll."

I stood up, and we walked down the hall.

"Seems like you guys had an interesting talk," Peter said.

"Yeah, no shit," I replied, "She said—"

"I'll take it from here, Officer Peter," a third voice echoed down the dim hallway.

I looked down the hall to see that familiar figure standing as still as a statue.

"Wouldn't want our prisoner losing his way, would you?"

The figure stepped out of the shadows and revealing Nigel and those hellfire eyes of his.

"What are you doing here, Nigel?" Peter asked, "You are supposed to be stationed at the cell."

"Oh come now, it's just little ol' Justin here, I'm sure that he's not going anywhere or going to make a run for it. This is his home. Isn't that right?" Nigel said, looking at me.

"This is not his home. I can get him where he needs to be," Peter said, grabbing me by the arm. "You've done enough already."

"Whatever do you mean, Officer?" Nigel asked, walking toward us. "My job is to guard and protect Mr. McMullen. Even if it means I have to protect him from himself."

"Protection?" Peter asked, "The word I would choose is a hindrance. He'd be safer with me."

"I'm not here to argue with you, Peter," Nigel said, pulling out his nightstick, "We both wouldn't want that. After seven long years of service in this prison, it would seem that you don't remember your place here anymore. Now if you would be so kind—"

"No," Peter said, "I'll escort the prisoner to his cell, and you will continue to watch over him for the night. Or have you forgotten the routine? You seem to remember everything else. Maybe you are having an off day?"

There was a brief silence as the two stood there, staring at each other for several moments. Neither one could stand the other, and they would let each other know it. Since the two have met, this war between them seems to have no end. It was like they have been at this before I was even born.

"I suggest you remind yourself of the limitations of your authority here, Officer Peter. It'll make things run smoother around here," Nigel said threateningly.

"Oh," Peter said, "And how do you figure that, Nigel?"

"Fact of the matter is Justin knows who the actual guard in here is and who is just the help. You are nothing more than someone who takes him on his little walks to see the lawyer that comes in here every morning. Do you think giving a sense of false hope to a prisoner doing a life sentence makes you some kind righteous hero? That's wishful thinking. It's pathetic."

"You wouldn't comprehend righteousness is if it bit you in the ass," Peter said, "I have to get him to his cell. So you get to be a good boy and watch him for tonight as always."

"Man, it just burns you up inside, doesn't it? Knowing that I am the one he listens to," Nigel retorted, "I have the authority here. If you have a problem with it, that's too bad. Those are the rules around here. It has been that way since this fine establishment was built."

"That's why you are here, isn't it?" Peter said, "Are you feeling a little lonely? Do you feel inadequate when your voice isn't the only one heard?"

"You tell me...you'd seem to be very familiar with that sensation, wouldn't you?" Nigel spoke up, strolling up to us.

"I'd say the word fits you so much better than it ever did me, Officer. Let me give you a little warning. Everything changes at some point. Soon you will wake up to that reality. Might be even sooner than you think," Peter said with a smirk.

Nigel looked in my direction. I put my head down, trying to avoid eye contact with him.

"Well, that day isn't going to be today, or anytime soon, I'm afraid...He is serving a life sentence. The prisoner is under my watch. And even though you may wear a badge, I highly recommend that you remember your position here. Your role. Now make yourself useful and take your goddamn hands off of my prisoner."

"Peter," I said, "Enough. Just let me go. Let him take me."

"Why?" Peter shot back at me.

"Just let him take me," I replied plainly, walking toward Nigel.

"Thank you, Justin." Nigel said, "Even the prisoner agrees. Now, would you be so kind as to let him go so we can all go about our day? You're being a hindrance, as you like to say."

Peter released my arm slowly. Nigel promptly grabbed my arm, yanking me to his side.

"Thank you, Officer," Nigel said, "I knew you would see it my way. I'll take the prisoner to his cell. He can tell me all about his talk today with the lawyer lady who came by. Did you ever get her real name, by the way, Justin?"

"No. No, I didn't," I replied.

"Oh? How can you trust someone who won't even give you her name? Isn't this lady supposed to get you out here? That doesn't sound fishy to anyone else?"

Nigel began walking me down the hall.

"Justin!" Peter yelled.

I turned and looked at him.

"Ms. Lawyer will be here tomorrow. Remember that. "

I nodded and continued to walk down back to my cell.

Nigel stopped in his tracks to turn and face Peter.

"This prisoner belongs here. No amount of small talk with some nameless bitch is going to change that," Nigel said, casually pulling the prison keys from his pocket.

"Does it ever occur to you that those keys that you are holding right now were given to you?" Peter asked, "They can be taken away. You may have power in here, now. I'll give you that. But everything will come to light at some point, Nigel. We both know that."

"Yeah?" Nigel asked, "You talk and act as if you were absent all those days. You're going to keep pretending like you didn't see or hear the things that created these walls? That persistent delusion of yours has always been a trait I've never been fond of."

"We'll see about that now, won't we?" Perter asked in an aggressive tone, peering indirectly at Nigel

"Always do," he replied tenaciously.

A Hint of Betrayal.

I walked back down the hallway to my cell with Nigel following close behind. The words that Ms. Lawyer stated were glued into my head.

I needed to watch what I allowed to be around me.

Maybe there was some truth to that. Talking to her about my brothers and my experiences was eye-opening. I never had to explain it to anyone previously openly. I started to believe that things could have been different. I had read in one letter that I skimmed through before I stopped accepting them, revealing that Jordan had gotten married. His wife gave birth to a girl named Alaia. I always wanted a sister when I was little since it was just us three boys. Mom often spoke about how disappointed she was that she didn't have a daughter of her own. I'm sure that she was ecstatic when Alaia was born. Did she have hazel eyes like my brother? How did her laugh sound? Would I even have a chance to hold her?

I had a soft spot for children. I considered myself as a kid at heart, and that made being around them a natural fit.

Me, an uncle?

Just the thought of her calling me Uncle Justin or Uncle Jay for the first time warmed my heart. I would explain to her how she had to be thirty years old before she could have a boyfriend. I'd go out to buy her an arcade stick to teach her how to play fighting games. However, that also meant that I would have to deal with my family again. There could be more fighting between us. I wasn't prepared to deal with that yet. I didn't want her to be around any fighting, but I was sacrificing the chance of never seeing her grow up.

I realized that I wanted kids of my own. Once high school was complete, I planned to find a decent job. Find a pretty and caring wife, have about three kids, and move away. We could all live happily in a lavish house with a swimming pool in the backyard. I would have my own office where I could write the stories that I always wanted to. My wife would knock on the door, then come in with a robe to hand me coffee. She would complain that I was working too much, kiss me on the cheek and tell me to go to bed. My kids and I would have great relationships. They'd be more intelligent and successful than I was. My wife and I would teach them good morals and how to be stand up individuals. I'd have one daughter whom I could spoil to death. I'd watch all of them grow up and have their own children. That way, I could be the youngest looking grandfather in the world since aging didn't seem interested in me. Jordans' lucky ass beat me to the punch. Maybe if Ms. Lawyer got me—

"Got you out of what?" Nigel asked as he was reaching for the keys on his side.

"Nothing," I said, "I wasn't thinking about anything."

Nigel opened the door cell and pointed in the room.

"Get in there," he ordered.

I slowly walked in. I noticed that it was a little brighter in here than usual.

"Hey, do you notice that—"

A large foot slammed into my chest and lifted me off of my feet. I felt myself vomiting before I hit the ground. As I landed, the back of my head hit the edge of the bed. I held my head, yelling in pain. Nigel walked up to me and grabbed me by my hair. He lifted me in the air as he landed several blows to my face before tossing me back to the ground.

"Y'know, I'm coming to the realization that this is going to have to be a routine with us until you shape the hell up," Nigel said. "It pains me to see you like this."

I tried to crawl away from Nigel. He walked to the side of me and stomped on my hand. He kicked me in the side with his black shoes and elbowed me in the middle of my back.

"But, you just refuse to listen to reason, don't you?" Nigel said. "I told you not to let that woman get in your head. Now you're losing focus."

"I'm not," I said, spitting out blood, "She is just trying to... trying to..."

"Shut up," he said, rolling me over on my back with his foot, "I wasn't finished speaking yet. You were thinking about leaving for the outside world again. I could've sworn that we were on the same page after our last conversation. I guess a quick history lesson is in order. You know all those people that you think about? They are going about their lives, not knowing or caring about what you did for them. Don't you recall the many times you had to be the adult in a room full of grown-ups that, by all rights, should have been able to take care of themselves? NO? Well, how about all the lies that hurt you as bad as they did? Or how about the months you had issues scraping to pay rent, to eat. Low and behold your loved one who was living with you had the nerve to walk in with a brand new outfit and shoes like everything was all peachy."

"I remember," I said, wiping the blood from my mouth. "I was weak. I should have done more."

"Not weak. Foolish. That's what you were. Plain and simple. You don't get a badge of honor for being a fool. They can tell you all day that you are helping the family and in the same breath, they're knifing you in damn back. Do you think that son of a bitch Peter is your friend? I am your friend. I'm the only friend you have."

Nigel sat on the edge of my bed.

"I feel sorry for you, kid. I do," he said. "It's like God made you the punch line to a shitty joke. You quietly dragged the burdens for everyone else's mistakes that you claim to love, while he is blessing them with the gifts you have yearned for years. Your brother is married now and has a beautiful daughter. Ain't that some shit? You wanted to marry at one point, didn't you? You wanted to claim your own little castle in the world. You wanted a sexy wife that you could put it to every night and have some beautiful kids, but you constantly made an effort to be altruistic. Admirable, if not misguided."

I stood up to my feet and leaned against the wall. I could barely feel face. My heart was beating rapidly and wouldn't stop.

"Of all the crimes you've committed, your foolishness is one of your greatest. You may have a big heart, which is something that you can never seem to let go of," Nigel said, chuckling, "However, there indeed lays the punch line, my friend. They don't mix with you. You were the good son. You were a loyal friend. Now, look at ya. Why does all this continue to happen?

I'm here to give you a little newsflash on why that is."

Nigel walked up to me and rammed his fist in the stomach this time. I bent over, feeling as if I was about to throw up my guts. He grabbed me by my shirt and put us face to face.

"Because you're a damn nobody. That's why."

Nigel pushed me back on the wall. He adjusted his shirt and tie.

"Once again, I have to apologize to you. As much as I hate having to beat common sense into you, it is the only way to make sure you don't repeat the same mistakes. It's a place that neither one of us wants to go back to. Brings up more questions that you shouldn't have to go through the trouble of answering," Nigel said, grabbing the keys from his pocket. "I knew I sensed a hint of betrayal. Betrayal is a trait you don't carry. You wouldn't betray a friend, would you?"

I shook my head.

Nigel opened the cell door. As he was about to walk out, he stopped.

"From now on, anytime you see the lawyer, I will consider it as a slap in the face. Try to comprehend when you're being lied to. No matter how many memories she makes you reflect on, she's not doing you any favors."

Nigel walked out of the cell door and slammed it closed.

"Sleep, Prisoner."

I limped over to my bed, holding the side of my face. I grabbed the grey blanket at the end of the bed and placed it over me. The warmth of the blankets gave little comfort. Nothing could. The brightness that I thought I had seen when I walked

72

into the cell was gone, as if it realized that it had come to the wrong place.

How did I let this happen? Maybe I was some punchline of a joke that God had made. Why would he put me on this Earth only to be jealous of the ones he meant to share life with? I was a fool wondering what life could be instead of accepting it as what it was. This place was all that I had.

What the hell was I thinking? Leaving wasn't an option. Ms. Lawyer had failed. There was nothing more to it than that. Reflecting on the past wasn't going to alter anything. If anything, it just reinforced that the same mistakes would come and repeat. I'd still be some nobody. Nigel was right again—There is no reward in staying a fool.

Pen and Paper

Three weeks had passed since that incident.

I stopped seeing the lawyer as Nigel had ordered. Peter had come the following day after the beating that I took from Nigel. Nigel lied, telling him that I had refused to see Ms. Lawyer. He added that I was going to carry out the rest of my sentence without ever fighting the case. The prison returned to its previous state. Peter would bring the mail, and Nigel would rip them up. Nigel went back to his usual self, not bothering threatening me again after what happened. Nigel was so confident that I wouldn't be a problem anymore that he rarely came to the cell in the evenings. He would walk to the cell and have his red eyes fixated on me for a few moments. He'd have a grin on his face once he had his fill and headed off into the main hallway.

I was sure that Ms. Lawyer was livid that she wasted her time, but there were others out there that needed her help. She's a dependable lawyer. Winning another case was going to be easy for her. Peter still wouldn't give up. He would come to say the usual good morning, give me a thumbs up, then go about his business. He never seemed defeated when I declined seeing Ms. Lawyer. My usual routine returned to the way it was. I'd wake up, do a few exercises, have the usual brief chat with the officers, and head to bed when I got tired.

It was unusually quiet this morning. Peter wasn't guarding the cell as he usually did at this hour. I walked to the cell door and tried to look down the hallway. No one was there.

"Nigel? Peter?" I called out.

No reply. As I walked away from the door, I heard paper slid-ing across the ground beneath my boot. I lifted my foot to find a white envelope on the ground.

"What the hell?" I said as I picked up the envelope, "I thought I told them to get rid of these."

I tossed the envelope on the ground and sat back on my bed, looking at the ceiling. The envelope stayed on my mind for a few minutes. Usually, these letters would come in droves, but this time it was just one single one. I got up from my bed and grabbed the envelope off the ground. I slowly walked to the cell door and peeped out, looking for signs of Nigel. When I saw that the coast was clear, I sat down on the floor and opened it. There was a folded piece of notebook paper. Written on it neatly was a message written in red ink.

Hey bro,

This is Cameron. I know that you are going through a lot. I hope that you can work through it so that you can get home soon. Jordan and I miss you. We all do. We need you here, baby bro. Stay safe.

I folded back the letter and placed it back in the envelope. I grabbed the top of the envelope about to tear it into two, but I stopped as I stood up. Walking over to my bed, I placed the let-ter in my pillowcase. I thought about writing Cameron back and just saying hello, telling him that I was okay. I was anxious as hell to ask about Alaia. I hadn't seen her with my own eyes. Just to see a picture would make all the difference in the world.

"You don't get to determine that!" I heard someone yelling

down the hall.

"Why do you keep putting him through this crap? It's pretty obvious he doesn't want the damn letters, so why even give them to him?"

"He has a right to choose that for himself! So open the door and then back the hell off!"

The gate at the end of the hallway opened, followed by footsteps. Peter walked up to the cell and knocked on the bars.

"Hey, sorry about the noise down there," he said, "More mail for you. You may rip it up as always, but you know, I have to do my job."

"That's fine," I said, "Leave them here. I'll take care of them."

"Oh...Okay," Peter said, placing the mail on the ground and walking away.

"Peter, just a sec," I said, rushing to the cell door. "I have to ask a favor. Can you get me paper and a pen when you can? There is someone that I want to write to."

Peter was stunned at my request, staring at me with his eyes wide open.

"Is this a prank?" he seemingly whispered to himself in disbelief, "You haven't asked anything from me in years. Excuse me if my hearing is getting worse, but did you just ask for a paper and pen?"

"Look, I don't want to go into detail. I just need a pen and paper. Can you do that for me?" I asked.

"A-all right! Of course. Yeah, I'll be back shortly. Hang on a second." Peter said, turning to briskly stroll down to the gate at the end of the hall.

As I waited for Peter to return, I reached back into the pillowcase to grab the letter that Cameron had sent and reread it. Words poured into my head. There was plenty that I could write in the message. The gate at the end of the hallway opened once more. Peter showed up with one pen and a stack of blank white papers.

"Here you go."

"Appreciate it," I nodded, reaching up as he handed them to me.

"Let me know if you need anything else," Peter said.

"I will. Thanks again."

I placed the stack of white papers on my lap. I took the pen in my hand and started to write my letter in blue ink.

Hey Bro,

I have so much to tell you since I have been away. I have much explaining to do—

I stopped writing. I didn't want to say too much about what I was doing in here, least of all, anything about Nigel. I balled up the letter and threw it to the ground. I decided that I'd write a simple reply.

Hey Cam,

I'm okay, bro. Sorry that I've been MIA this long. I'll do my best to keep you up to date as often as I can. Thank you for the letter and any others that you sent.

—Justin

I folded up the two letters and put them into my pillowcase

as neatly as possible. I stuffed the pen that I had in my sock. I didn't want to leave any signs, or Nigel would suspect that something was up.

I waited for Peter to show up the next day. When I heard the gate down the hallway open, I hurried to grab the letter that I had written and stood by the cell door.

Peter walked over, carrying more mail.

"Got some more mail for you, sir," Peter said.

"Listen, Peter. I have another favor to ask," I told him, handing him the letter that I wrote. "From now on, I'm going to be sending messages to my older brother, Cameron. I was hoping you could make sure that they are being sent to him. I will only accept letters from him from here out. "

"You got it," Peter replied cheerfully, "I'll make it happen."

"Thank you. Make sure that Nigel doesn't know about them, please," I said, "This is going over his head, but I don't want him finding out about this."

Peter gave me a salute gesture. He placed the letter inside his blue button-up shirt and walked down the hallway, whistling joyfully.

Over the next few weeks, my older brother and I continued to exchange letters. He explained how he was trying to get his music career on track. He spoke about his now seven-year-old son, Zion, whom I hadn't seen since he was one. In one letter, he sent a picture of Alaia; She had beautiful light skin, big brown eyes, and a puffy Afro. She looked so much like Jordan that they were practically twins. He informed me that Jordan and Alaia were inseparable. Jordan carried her wherever he went, and she was now laughing at anything that he did. She had her first birthday party, which Jordan had thrown for her. My niece and nephew were growing up fast, but I could never answer when he asked me to come home. I couldn't continue reading a letter when he would write: "home wasn't the same without me being there." I didn't know how to reply, so I would ignore it and ask about something else.

Talking to my brother once more enabled me to look forward to the next day for once. I was still a prisoner, but I felt that I had at least fixed a relationship with my brother that was long overdue.

Face to Face

"Here at last," Peter said, rushing to the door at the end of the hallway. He opened it, finding Ms. Lawyer waving at him.

"Good evening, Peter," she said, "Thank you for allowing me an audience at such short notice."

"And how could I not? You always lighten up the place. We could use some of that around here now and then," Peter said. He closed the door and walked with her down the hallway.

"Oh, Peter," she said, "Still so kind and flattering after all these years. You are too good to me. Is Mr. McMullen awake?"

"Yes, ma'am. I'm grateful that you agreed to see him," Peter said. "He started accepting some letters from his older brother. They have been writing to each other for about two weeks now, consistently. I figured that would have softened him up by now, so you could talk some sense into him."

"Let's hope your assumption is correct," she replied.

"The prisoner will not be taking any visitors at this time," a voice cut into the conversation. "As he requested a month ago, he is no longer seeking to fight his sentence."

Nigel stood in the hallway in front of the gate that led to Justin's cell. He was holding the keys firmly in one hand with his other clenched into a fist.

"Well now, look who finally decided to say hello," Ms. Lawyer said.

"What the hell do you think you are doing, Peter? Why is she here?" Nigel questioned, disgruntled.

"I'm here on my own accord. I wish to speak to Mr.McMullen

about his case. Now would you be so kind as to let me through, please?" Ms. Lawyer asked.

"I wouldn't be so kind as a matter of fact," Nigel replied, taking a few steps toward Ms. Lawyer, " And I have an issue with repeating myself. My prisoner is peacefully serving his sentence. I would hate for him to be upset by your falsehoods."

"Nigel, please move out of the way," Peter asked, placing his hand on Nigel's shoulder to move him.

Nigel pushed Peter away into the wall behind him.

"You close your damn mouth!" Nigel pointed at Peter, with his eyes stretched open. "You have been warned before!"

"Gentlemen!" Ms. Lawyer yelled. "I am not here to break up a confrontation. I understand the quarrel between you, but I request that you don't do anything rash."

Peter brushed off his shirt and stood up straight off the wall.

"Peter, my dear," Ms. Lawyer said softly. "May I have a moment with Officer Nigel, please? I want to discuss some matters with him if I may."

"Are you sure? My co-worker seems a little worked up this evening. Wouldn't want his anger to put you in an uncomfortable situation." Peter said.

"I will be fine, I'm sure. Won't I, Officer...Nigel?" Ms. Lawyer asked.

Nigel grunted as he crossed his arms, his posture signaling the tolerance of her presence.

Peter slowly walked past Nigel, staring him down as he went by.

"Thank you, Officer Peter, for your understanding," Ms. Lawyer said.

A brief moment of silence seemed to cause even time to stop as Ms. Lawyer, and Nigel stood there, eyes locked.

"...Face to face again," said Mrs. Lawyer, "You go by the name Nigel in here, huh? It's much better than what you normally get."

"Funny. I don't share the same fondness for your new name. 'Ms. Lawyer' was the best you could come up with?" Nigel replied.

"Well, seeing how this is a prison, I felt it was fitting. You seem to have a lot more power here than I thought," She admitted with sarcastic praise. "He has given himself almost fully to your influence."

"I'm doing him a favor. The way I see it, I'm sparing him of any further disappointments."

"You think that keeping him in that cell is helping him, Nigel? You are doing nothing but submitting him to this dark, disgusting place. Don't pretend that you are some guardian with me. You may be able to pull that with others that you have affected over time, but as always, I see right through it."

"And that makes you think that you will save this one? If that's what you believe, you are just adding fuel to the fire; You and Peter are nothing but instruments of the biggest lie that has been around since the beginning of mankind. Some unfortunate few make it past me, sure. But we both know what's come to pass in his life. You've seen it. So I can't fathom the notion that you are trying to save anyone. No amount of bullshit that you spit at him will change the elements that are and will always be at play in his life."

Ms. Lawyer simply shook her head at him.

"Poor, little negative man," she said. "Misery just loves company. Speaking of that, Peter told me that he noticed Justin had a few bumps and bruises that he didn't want to tell him about from a few weeks ago. Do you care to explain? I'm sure you have some justification for the moment."

"Prisoners need to be kept in line from time to time, don't they? Nuff said." Nigel retorted bluntly. "I can't be blamed for wanting to keep things as they ought to be...and having the will to do so. You have no control here."

"You don't know the meaning of control. Your behavior will be nothing more than a detriment to his growth and anyone that allowed you to be around them," Ms. Lawyer replied."

"Detriment...You like to parrot your peers, it seems. If you were any good at your job, I wouldn't be here. WE wouldn't even be here. You're more responsible than I am." Nigel scoffed.

They shared another exchanged glare that filled the hall with a bitter silence.

"He needed to remember why he's here. I did what I do best, that's all. Remind those that need to be reminded. That's more than anything you or that optimistic clown have ever done."

"Oh, I agree, Nigel," Ms. Lawyer said. "You are an essential part of this person that you are watching so closely. He does need you. Contrary to popular belief, I want you here."

Nigel slightly shook his head in the manner that a disappointed parent would when scolding a child.

"No...no, no, no...no." Nigel huffed with a hint of amusement of trading nuanced barbs with her. "Don't mock me, bitch. Your little games won't save you here. This place belongs to me now. It is just as much as my prison as it is his."

"And that's where the hole in your plan is; You know I don't 'play games.' I genuinely believe that you are the best thing that has happened to him. Once this is all over, you are going to be the sole reason why everything in this godforsaken place crumbles," Ms. Lawyer spoke firmly and confidently.

"...That's it. That's your plan, huh?" Nigel walked toward Ms. Lawyer, rubbing the side of his face. "To get him to believe in himself? To get him to want to leave here and never come back? I'll tell you what. Tell him all the sweet words that you want. Build him up with illusions that things will improve, and send him out on his merry way. I won't have to lift a finger. We'll just let humanity play out. It'll be your fault when he falls apart again. Yours. Don't act confused when Justin's beyond your reach, Faith."

"No," Ms. Lawyer said, "The illusion is that he will stay within yours."

One More Try

"Hello, Mr. McMullen."

I jumped at the sound of the voice that I heard. Ms. Lawyer was standing in front of my cell. I still couldn't see her face, but I could feel a smile come over mine.

"That's the first time I have ever seen you make that expression. You must have missed me," Ms. Lawyer said.

"What are you doing here?" I asked half perplexed, half surprised.

"I am here to continue with the development of our defense," she said, "Why else would have come here? This place is not what I consider welcoming."

"I thought that you gave up on it after I declined to see you,"

"That's one thing that you should know by now about me, Mr. McMullen," Ms. Lawyer carried a sense of trust as she spoke, "I don't give up, and I'm hoping that you will share that mindset with me for a few more days."

I stood up off of my bed.

"Listen, I'm happy that you want to help me. I am. But I am just worn out with all of this. I have been this way for a very long time. If you read all of those files, you should understand that. I don't need this to repeat anymore."

"I do understand that. I understand your crimes, sir, but I do not believe that you owe the rest of life to them. I have represented many people. I've seen many things. Some have given up on themselves, saying that their situation is too big to get out of. I don't believe that, Mr. McMullen. Everyone goes through a storm. Life can throw many things at you, never stopping no matter how bad things get. You have to learn that you have to face those issues, not yield to them."

"You don't get it," I said, "Who I am got me in here."

"And what you can become can get you out if you believe that you can be better than this. How about this? Commit to going over these last three files. Just take a look at why I believe that you are innocent."

"So what if it doesn't work?" I asked.

"That depends entirely on if you want it to or not," she replied, "Come on. Just one more try."

Ms. Lawyer's personality reminded me a lot of a few of my cousins that I grew up with named Novi and Jerry. No matter how I acted, they never gave up on me. At one point in my life, I even tried to avoid them too. They admired me, but I didn't get why. We hardly saw each other. I wouldn't even make an effort to see them. I begin to wonder if I didn't get the concept of family or somewhere along the way I had lost it.

Why would she go this far for someone like me? I was still a nobody. Someone who had just quit on life, but maybe that was what held me back all these years.

I told myself I was nobody too many times.

I accepted it. Perhaps it was time that I faced this storm once more.

"You don't give up, do you?" I asked.

"It's not in my DNA," Ms. Lawyer replied with her brows raised and conviction in her voice, "Let's get you out of here."

THE THIRD CHAPTER
The Long Walk

I accompanied Ms. Lawyer and Peter to the interrogation room. I couldn't help thinking about Nigel. It was funny that every time that I thought about leaving here, all I could think about was him. I've taken a beating from him in the past, but he was more determined than ever to keep me here. Since Ms. Lawyer has shown up, the prison atmosphere had changed even when I agreed not to see her. Hope is something that I gave up on a long time ago.

Some things never change, no matter how bad we want them to.

I waited for the day when I was young that I would grow up to be this big strong, attractive man. One day while driving to school, my dad asked me about my grades. He asked, "If you remain this way in when you go to high school, what will you do?" I told him that I was going to be a famous basketball player. When he asked what would happen if that didn't work, I had some delusional answer, not thinking about what I was saying. The point is that I've always had dreams.

When did I lose sight of them?

My train of thought was interrupted when we started to approach Nigel, who was leaning against the hallway wall with his arms crossed. He was staring directly at me, ignoring Ms. Lawyer and Peter. He didn't say a thing as I walked passed him, but that alone said a million damn words. I had betrayed him. I listened to Nigel's warnings for years. Now for the first time in a while, I was looking to someone else for answers. I had just committed to proving my innocence.

"Just focus on getting to the interrogation room, Justin," Peter said, "You are making the right decision."

We reached the door to the interrogation room. Peter opened the door, then signaled Ms. Lawyer and me to come in. As I followed Ms. Lawyer's lead into the room, I turned to look back at Nigel, who was now standing straight up in the middle of the hallway staring back at me. His fists were locked, and he was as still as the air around us. There was almost an aura that you could see flowing around him.

"Justin," Peter said, placing his hand on my shoulder, "Please enter the room to begin the meeting. I will be just outside the door just in case you two need me."

I nodded and headed inside. Ms. Lawyer walked to her seat and pulled out a red folder titled "File #3," and Blue folder titled "File #4" and placed them on the table.

I pulled back the silver steel chair and sat down.

"That was quite the long walk," she said, "Officer Nigel's 'strong personality' could suck the air out of the Earth, I swear. He is quite the character."

"Yeah, tell me about it," I said.

"Wow...You were running to his defense before whenever I bad mouthed him," Ms. Lawyer said curiously. "Did anything happen between you two that I should be aware of?"

"No," I said. "Nothing—"

"Cut the crap," She said, cutting me off, "You come in here with bruises all over you. You're not in your cell, beating yourself to a pulp. Self-inflicted crimes charges or not, I doubt that you are unstable enough to do that. How long?"

"How long what?" I asked.

"How long has this been going on?" Ms. Lawyer asked.

"Pretty much since I made it in here," I explained, "When you showed up the second time, that's when he attacked me again."

"Did you fight back?" Ms. Lawyer asked. "Do you let him assault you?"

"What do you expect me to do against him? Kick his ass? Beat him up and take the keys? I can't do that, and you know it."

"So, you lay there and take it?"

"What the hell are you getting at?"

"You know, Mr. McMullen, I have noticed a common trait in many people. Most are quick to make excuses when someone or something abuses them for a long period. They are also much quicker to getting angry when someone challenges them to face their troubles. Do you know why that is?"

"I'm sure that you are going to tell me," I said sarcastically.

"Because they have accepted it. That's why. You have accepted that these occurrences will continue, so instead of fighting it, you surrender to it. You don't even think of defending yourself. The abuse you have taken has built up within you for so long that you believe that you are always going to be a victim. Has that idea ever occur you? Have you ever tried to fight through a storm?"

"I can't say that I have yet," I said, sitting back in my chair.

"I'm glad that you admit that. I have learned that the first step in fixing a problem is admitting that there is one," She stated, giving a quick glance at her notes. "Today is going to be a little bit different. We will be going over two files in this meeting. I have learned quite a lot about you, and we are ready to dive a little bit into our defense. There are two periods in time that I want to review with you. We will be focusing on your sophomore year of high school and the summer of that year. Do you recall those years, sir?"

"I do. That was the year where I was with Bee." I said.

"I have read a bit about this Bee of yours. Can you tell me a little about her?" Ms. Lawyer asked.

"She was a girl that I dated off and on. She started as my best friend, then naturally, it turned into something more."

"So you did have a girlfriend at some point? You made it seem that you were the ugliest thing in the universe and couldn't score one. She didn't seem to think so."

"She was the only one I thought would give me the time of day,"

"Why is that?" Ms. Lawyer asked.

"What do you—You know why! You didn't listen to me before?" I yelled out.

"I listened to you, but I don't believe for a second that every single girl in the school dismissed you or paid no attention to you. With that said, why did you measure the quality of yourself as a person by what women think about you?" Ms. Lawyer asked, crossing her arms.

"I don't know to be honest," I said, "It's a combination of

things. Peer pressure, not feeling wanted. When you finally do get attention, you run with it."

"Bingo," Ms. Lawyer said, scooting her chair up to the table, "The plot thickens. The answer that I've been dying to hear! Okay, let's discuss 2006. You were in your sophomore year. As always, every little detail helps."

File #3
The Birds and the Bee

As I talked about in File #1, in the 8th grade, I had attended Jefferson Middle School. While I didn't make the basketball team that year, it was much more enjoyable overall than before. That year I attended Jefferson with my younger brother, Jordan, who quickly made his presence known. There were times where I had to get him out of trouble, but it was fun attending a school with him again.

At the beginning of the year, I played basketball with a group of friends behind the school. When I had sat down to rest after a game, I looked to my right and saw one of the most beautiful girls that I have ever seen in my life. She had amazing brown skin and a well-shaped figure. She had on a white tee shirt and pink shorts. The smile that she gave me shook my core.

At that time, I would never approach a girl like that because I knew my nerves would get better when I talked. I would start shaking, and my stomach would start hurting. This time though, there was something different about this one. When she continued to walk past me, I looked back at her, causing me to double-take as I was hit with a full glimpse of her figure. In my head, she was just too beautiful to let walk away. The way she strolled was incredible to me. It was like God had made her with all my preferences in mind. This time I told myself, "Look, man, forget this, I need to know her name right now." I ran to her as fast as I could.

"Dang, you move fast!" I said when I reached her.

She giggled, continuing to walk down the sidewalk.

"What do you want?" she asked as if to humor me, "I need to get home."

"Okay, you can, but can you give me your name first?"

"It's Bee," she said lightheartedly, "Am I allowed to go home now?"

"I didn't even give you my name yet. It's Justin," I said, "I know that you didn't ask, but I wanted to tell you anyway."

"Okay, Justin, I'll remember that in the future. Are you going to let me go home now?"

"No," I said, "Come watch me play basketball."

"I'm sorry, but my mom expects me to be at home at this time," Bee said, widening that beautiful smile.

"And? Tell her you had to stay after school for homework. That's a lie that I tell all the time, and it works! "

"No, crazy boy, I have to go," she said, laughing, "I'm sure that I will see you again soon."

"Okay, you better," I said.

She turned and waved goodbye. I ran back to the basketball court where my little brother, Jordan, was.

"Yo, you know that Bee girl down there?" I asked him, pointing in her direction.

"Who?" Jordan asked, looking at where I was pointing, "Oh yeah, I know her. Everybody likes her, man."

"I see why. She was fine as hell. I need her number, man," I said, rubbing my hands together, "That could be the new girlfriend!"

"Go get her then, bro!" Jordan egged me on.

I wouldn't see Bee for days after that. I kept an eye out for her at school. I was always wondering what she was doing. I was determined that the next time I saw her that I was going to get her number. The funny thing was, fate must have heard my cry, and on a Friday morning, I saw her again. My parents had driven my brothers and me to school. Once we were parked, my mother called out to a girl that was walking into the building. The girl turned around, and sure enough, there was Bee. She ran to the car to hug my mother. I rolled down my window and smiled at her. She had a surprised look on her face.

"This is your mom?" Bee asked me half stunned.

"Yups, this be my mamas," I responded playfully, "How do you know her?"

"Her mom is my friend," my mother said.

My eyes lit up. I couldn't believe it. This was the girl I was digging at the time, but our mothers were also friends. The situation was too perfect. I was going to make my move soon. About a week later, I got a chance to meet Bee's mother. Her mother was beautiful, just like Bee. She always had this big smile that made her a pleasure to have around. I could tell that she was a caring mother. She was a phenomenal cook too. They had a white and blue colored house that was well within walking distance of mine. I would come to visit Bee as much as I could throughout the school year. We would play her Nintendo Game-Cube. We discovered that we had a lot of common interests. We both loved fantasy shows, Super Mario, and she kept up with any new games. Slowly but surely, we began to develop a bond. She became my best friend.

Whenever I was in class, she would come by and peek through the door to see me. For the life of me, I never learned how she found out my class schedule, but I didn't care. It was flattering to have someone to care enough to see how you were doing.

While I was at her house, I had built up the courage to finally ask her to be my girlfriend. I was ready. I sat her down, prepared to make my move.

"Hey there, ol' buddy. We seem to be getting a lot closer lately," I said, rubbing the top of my head nervously.

"Yes, we have," she said.

"Sooooo, I was wondering. Would you like to be my girl-friend? There I said it,"

Bee gave a deep breath.

"Look, Justin. We can go out for one week to see what happens. If I don't like it, we are breaking up."

That wasn't the greatest answer in the world, but what the hell, it was better than no, and it was a victory nonetheless. I hugged then kissed her on the cheek. We talked on the phone every day that week. Bee started to open up to me even more, telling me more about her family history, what her father was like, and some of the problems that she came across in school. She was a big Harry Potter fan, and while I wasn't big into that franchise at the time, I attempted to learn more about it. I liked what she liked, so I made it a mission to watch all the Potter movies that were out at the time so that we would have something to talk about.

However, after that week, we had stopped talking for a few

months due to my grades slipping in a few classes. As usual, my parents weren't happy with it, so I was placed on a strict punishment. No video games or phones were allowed until the end of the 1st quarter of school, which stopped us from talking or seeing each other for almost a month.

The fall season of the school year arrived. One day, I was sitting at my computer doing homework for a class that I was growing frustrated with. The computer that I was working on was located close to the back door and the window. I heard voices outside the window, and when I looked up, Bee and her best friend were outside talking to my little brother. Bee looked at me and smiled, which changed my mood instantly. A few minutes later, she was gone. I called her that night asking her why didn't she come in and speak to me. She explained that she didn't want to bother me because I looked "pissed at the world."

We continued to talk throughout the months after without ever breaking contact. Whenever I woke up or walked into the living room, nine times out of ten, Bee would be there. She would watch me play basketball on the street corner when I played with some of the kids around the neighborhood. One of those days, as she watched me play, I decided that I was going to go in for the kill.

I was going to get my first kiss from her.

When one of the games ended, I sat next to her on the corner.

"Yo," I said, "How's it going over here?"

"Hot. I need to get some water," Bee said, wiping the sweat from her head.

"Don't worry. I will get you one in a sec. Hey um, I wanted to ask something. Why haven't you kissed me yet?"

Bee looked at me and laughed.

"What do you mean?" she said.

"I mean, we have been talking for a while, and you ain't even laid one on me yet. Don't you think it's about to be that time?"

"Shouldn't we just wait until it happens, Justin?" she asked, giving me that big smile that was to die for.

"You right, you right, you right," I said, shaking my head up and down. "I guess we can wait for that perfect time. When would that be, I wonder? Hmm...how about now?"

Bee then gave me that deep stare that I would get lost in. Those brown eyes were my Kryptonite. I had never wanted anything in my life more at that time. As her face slowly headed toward mine, I got more and more excited. It wasn't that I was kissing a beautiful girl or that I had the girl with a fantastic body, but I was kissing my best friend. Then our lips touched for the first time. I fist-pumped in the air in celebration.

"You are so stupid," she said.

"How?" I asked. "That kiss was crazy. I finally got it. Finally! Hey...can I have another one?"

Our relationship hit another level after that. We started spending even more time together. The world seemed to be a better place with her around. When you are as young as we were at that age, you don't ever take relationships like the one I had with Bee seriously. I was in 8th grade, but I could happily say that was the first time I was in genuine love with a person. Just speaking, Bee's name was enough to get a goofy grin out of me. We stayed together for about a year after that, until I went to high school, but no one ever took the spot that only she had in my life.

This brings me to the year 2006 of my sophomore year of high school.

The year as I said before, was already going badly in every aspect. There were already many things that had eaten at my personality, so I wasn't the same person that I was when I had first gotten with Bee. I didn't have any luck with the ladies at all, so I was very lonely.

Somewhere along the line, I had started thinking about Bee again. We were in different schools then. But I told myself that I already had a girl who liked me, so there was no reason to talk to any other females at my school.

During the winter season of the school year, I decided to get back in contact with Bee. I had my younger brother try to talk to her for me because he still went to school with her. When he had returned with a verdict, he told me that she said that she didn't want to talk to me because we had stopped talking after we left middle school. She said that I was interested in other women and not her anymore, which was not valid. I was determined to have her back in my life again.

I got her number back from my mothers' cell phone and called her. We spoke briefly before I told her I wanted to see her again. We arranged a time that night when I would come over and talk to her. I was spending a night at my best friend's house that day, which was closer to Bees' home. His name was Napoleon, but we called him Poley. I rode my bike to her house around our scheduled time. When she came outside, she wore tight blue jeans, black knee-high boots, and a black fur jacket. Her hair was braided in a ponytail.

"Hi," she said, "How are you, stranger?"

I swear I didn't even recognize her voice, and she was right in front of me. There was something very different about this girl. She gave an air of confidence, more so than before. She was aware of her sex appeal, knowing that she had a body that not many girls could match at her age. Her posture was different. The way she moved had changed. But I had come to the house expecting that happy, fun-loving girl who would laugh at my jokes. What I got was someone that had a different flare. She still was attracted to me for sure, but this time the way she looked at me, exchanging kisses wouldn't be enough anymore.

"Hi, how are you? It's good to see you again, " I said.

"You're welcome," she said, circling me, "You came out in this cold just to see me, huh?"

"I was hoping that we could talk again. You know, start where we left off."

"Well, that is going to be tough because I'm talking to someone right now," she said.

"Oh, I didn't know that," I said, disappointed, "Should I go?"

"No. No," Bee said, "It's not serious. Stay. You came to see me, right?"

"Yeah, but are you guys like together?"

"I said that it wasn't that serious," she said.

Bee walked up to me and put her hands in my pockets. She gave me the first kiss that I had gotten from her in a long time.

This kiss wasn't the puppy love peck that you saw kids give each other in middle school. It was a deeper, longer kiss than usual. I know that all things change over time, but it had been about a year in a half since I was last with Bee. That kiss she gave me felt like we were just a few seconds away from something more. Each one that we shared was stronger than the last. Bee would let me touch her in places that she would've smacked me across the face if I had tried it before. She would say little things to me in my ear now. Telling me how much she wanted me to come inside the house with her so that we could be alone.

The whole thing took me by surprise. I was not ready for who Bee was when I got there, but that slowly changed as the night went along. She was so damn sexy. I wanted to go further with her then, but something in my mind told me not to do it. Whenever she asked me to come inside her house with her, I came up with any excuse I could. At the end of our time together, we shared our most intimate kiss. While I was kissing her, I placed my hands on her hips. She laughed as I was kissing her, took my hand, and put them over her butt. It was the first time that she let me do that. I knew what I wanted right at that moment. I wanted her back in my life more than ever now, and I would do anything to have her again, no matter what. I left and went back to Poley's house a few seconds after that.

The whole way back, all I could think about was Bee's body. I told Poley about what had happened after. He told me that I was getting "whipped" by her. I denied it then, but soon it sunk in that Poley's words may have been spot on.

I called Bee to ask her if I could see her again. She told me that that was a one-time deal. She said she was trying to show me that she was better than the girls that she thought that I was chasing in high school. I explained that I didn't want any of them and that she was the only person that I was chasing. She warned me that she wasn't the same Bee that I used to know. She felt that she was weak back then, feeling that she was always holding back who she was. I had never heard her speak that way before. It came off as cold. I chalked it up to her, still mad at me for not being able to talk to her when we went to separate schools.

I tried to explain to calm her down, but she wasn't too keen on hearing what I had to say. She hung up on me during the call. I was a little bummed by that, but it didn't stop me from talking to her. I found out about a month later that Bee had some Mexican boyfriend that she was really into. He was her first time, and naturally, she had deep feelings for him. I hated the guy despite not ever meeting him. I didn't care, though. He was not stopping me from getting with her. He was just in the way.

I tried what I could to get Bee's attention. I called her when I could to get her to talk to me, send her love letters, and everything I could to win her favor. One day, she decided that she would give me the time of day again. She called me out of the blue one night to speak. I did my best to explain why I liked her so much, but she said that she didn't know if she wanted to be with me again. We did, however, talk about what it would be like if we did get back together. She explained that if another relationship were to happen, another layer would have to be added to it.

Sex.

"You don't want to wait on that?" I asked her.

"Why should we wait?" she replied. "We both want it."

She told me how bad she wanted me since she was young. I had thought about it, of course, but in my head, it would be a little while before we got to that point. She told me what she wanted me to do to her. She became irresistible with every word she spoke. The more I heard, the more my desire for her grew. Bee asked me what I was doing the next day. She told me that she would be around my neighborhood tomorrow afternoon, and she wanted to come over. I told her that would be fine as my parents wouldn't be home.

The following day, I couldn't tell you how excited I was. Bee was about to come over again to see me. When she did, we went to my room, and I locked the door. We didn't have sex because we did not have protection, but I was finally able to touch under her clothes. She was so soft everywhere. The sounds that she made had me in a trance. But after we had enough playing around, we had sat down to discuss the idea of getting back together again, which she said she would give more thought to.

On a stormy day, while I was visiting Bee at her home, the two watched a movie. In the middle of it, Bee whispered in my ear, "I'm ready." She started to kiss me while rubbing my chest. I picked her up, carrying her into her bedroom. I took a condom out that I kept in my wallet. That day, I was ready too. It was the first time that Bee and I would go all the way.

I thought that I had finally found the love that I was looking for all of my life. It was a passionate experience, and who else to share it with but her? She told me after that she and her boy-friend were no longer dating, and it opened more time for us to spend together. So we became a couple again.

Sex became an everyday thing for us after that. I would come over to her house every day after school. As a seven-teen-year-old boy with a girlfriend with that hourglass figure you'd expect to see women have in a music video, it was the greatest thing in the world. We would talk to build up the ex-citement for the next time we would do it. After we were done, we'd talk about everything that happened in the bed. The sexual part of our relationship was everything that you could ask for. However, outside of those moments, our relationship became a problem that I didn't know how to cope with.

I underestimated what time could do to a person. Bee and I had issues with our relationship very early. It seemed as though the only thing we had going was our physical relationship. Most of the time, we did nothing but argue. There was no friendship anymore. She didn't like to do a lot of the activities that we used to, telling me that I was lame for even having an interest in them. There were constant lies that she would tell me. I'd come to visit her only to find pictures of her ex-boyfriend on her bed. I would hear rumors about different boys from even her close friends that were embarrassing for me as a boyfriend. At one point, I heard her say that we were never together to someone else.

Deep down, I knew that some of this information was true. It wasn't even in the sense that I believed them out of ignorance, the red flags were there plain as daylight. I realized the relationship that I was in was damaging mentally. I struggled with this, but I tried to do everything in my power to fix it, but nothing I did worked. Our mothers being best friends, did nothing to help the situation. My mother, in particular, had a massive issue with our relationship for some odd reason. She'd explain to me that Bee was no good and just some "fast ass little girl," which was completely different from how she acted toward Bee prior.

Throughout all of it, I still loved her. I always wanted no one else in the world except for her. That mindset came with a price. The real reason I stayed with Bee was to say I had someone. I had a chick with a great body and was good in bed. At the time, that was good enough for me no matter how disrespectful she was. There were many times when she wanted to break up with me. I ignored them, telling myself that we could work past our problems. This relationship carried on like this for eight grueling months.

My entire outlook on Bee would take a turn one night. I called her after I finished my homework. She answered the phone while talking on another phone to someone else. She was speaking Spanish to another guy that I was sure was her ex-boy-friend. I was so pissed off by some of the stuff that she said to the dude that I started yelling at her to stop talking to him. To this day, I believe that this was another setup to get me to break up with her. When she got on the phone with me, she told me that she wanted to get back with her ex.

Believe it or not, that was the least harming thing that she had said. She started to attack me as an individual, telling me that I was annoying because I was too much of a goody-two-shoes. She said that our relationship was boring to her. She needed someone who was able to speak to her a certain way. This conversation went on for the better part of an hour. Pleading my case to her didn't matter. Her mind was made up.

Our relationship ended that night. The one person that I felt I had a connection with was gone. I was left miserable for months. The friends that I had took issue with how I was acting. due to the breakup. I would start tearing up out of anger while yelling in my room when no one was around. I was furious at myself. I was so determined to have someone love me the way I thought I should be that I had allowed an individual to determine my happiness for me. The outcome of my whole day was determined by what she said to me. If she was happy with me at the moment, I was delighted. If she didn't feel like being bothered with me, my whole world would come crashing down.

I needed someone else to validate me. At that time, I anticipated the opportunity to show a person that I was worthy of the time of day. Still, disappointments in trying to achieve that became a common occurrence. I never realized that the love that I needed was the one that I overlooked the most.

The love for myself.

You

Ms. Lawyer hummed reflectively, "That's quite the tale."

"You asked," I said, smiling, "But, yup. That's what happened."

"You said something there at the end, Mr. McMullen, that caught my attention. I was even a little thrown off that you said it."

"What was that?" I asked.

"You said that the love that you needed most was your own. Tell me more about that."

"The relationship with Bee showed me that a lot was missing within myself. I didn't know who I was. How can someone love you when you don't even know who you are? When you go through a situation like that, you have to look in the mirror."

Mr. Lawyer started clapping her hands.

"Mr. McMullen," she started, "You've come quite some ways from where you were three weeks ago. I even heard that you have also been accepting mail from your older brother. How is he?"

"Good," I said, "He is doing well. He is taking care of himself and talks about his son, Zion, a lot. Says that he is getting bigger."

"That's great. I'm happy that you are taking mail now. It's always good to have someone to talk to and share things with. You and your older brother were close when you guys were very little, no?"

"We couldn't be separated. I used to cry when his Dad

would take him away for the weekend. I would grab on to him tight. I would fight his Dad's family whenever they would come for him," I said.

"That's right, you guys are half brothers?"

"Yeah, we have different fathers."

"I see. Touching back on the file we just discussed, I am happy that you acknowledged that there was a lack of self-respect. I understand your reasoning that you had at the time you were seeing Ms. Bee. You said plenty of times now that you wanted to feel appreciated. It is something that we all want and some will go extreme lengths to get that. Now that we have an understanding of what was missing, let's dive deeper into this. I'll begin with this question. Why do you hate yourself so much?" she asked.

"Because I felt that no one else outside my family liked me. I felt that I wasn't worthy of love. I never intended to think that way. One day it just snowballed out of control. As days went by, I just hated what I saw in the mirror," I said.

"Was that why you tried to stay with Bee when you knew it wasn't healthy?" She asked.

"Yes. It was like I had said before. I wanted someone to see something in me that I didn't see in myself. I thought that someone could bring that out of me. Now that I think about it, I wish I could have done it all over again. None of that shit would have ever happened."

"No. Everything happens for a reason. You made a mistake, and it took you a while, but you did learn from it. It is never too late to want to change. Bee had her own choices to make. Holding on to a grudge builds a wave of anger in you that harms only you in the long run. It places a wall that will keep anyone that cares about you from ever getting in."

"You're right," I said, "I held on to that for a while. A long ass time. It wasn't just with Bee. I was angry about who I was period. Then you always feel like a victim. In the back of your head, you believe that everyone is out to get you. "

"Believe me when I tell you it's easier said than done, but you have to let that go. You understand that, don't you? If you don't, you will continue to live in the past. Changing is making a decision that you want to change. It doesn't come overnight, but trying is always a good start."

I stood up out of my seat and began to pace back and forth.

"I tried that. I did. I always go back to that anger. I get bitter. I'm happy for a while, and then something happens that knocks all that shit back down," I said.

"Such is life, Mr. McMullen," She said. "It is full of tests. There will always be a blow that comes out of nowhere and knocks us all down. Life is not going to stop sending problems your way. You cannot outrun a storm. You have to face it."

"I know," I said, "It's the reason why I'm still here. I'm here because I ran for so long. Nigel was the only one that I could turn to. This prison blocks out the noise. It's quiet here. No one can bother me. I thought after a few years here, I'd find the answer. I was wrong about that as everything else."

"Mr. McMullen, I think that you have all the tools you need to better your life. This place is not for you. Being alone here is the same as giving up. Change has to start in one place, within you."

"I don't know if I can do that yet," I said, sitting back down, "I need more time. I need more time to figure stuff out."

"Of course, sir," Ms. Lawyer replied, "But don't let life pass you by before you decide to take action. Bee went a different way. She is living her life like everyone else you know. Isn't it time to start living yours?"

It has been so long since I've "lived." I was content being here in this prison. Ms. Lawyer's words were starting to reach me.

"Okay, who are you?" I asked her, "Really, though. I've never heard of a lawyer like you."

"Let's just say that I come from a very ambitious firm," she answered in a casually dismissive sense, "We take on cases most people give up on. All will be explained in due time. Let's continue. I hear that you are also a *Street Fighter* player."

I paused and then laughed in amusement.

"What? Are we going to use that in our defense?"

"Why not? I think it's a good idea," Ms. Lawyer said.

"What? Wait? We are going to use a fighting game as evidence in a courtroom?"

"Sure, we are going to take them by surprise," she said, "I want to talk about the summer of 2007 after Bee had left and moved out of state. There are two names that I want you to tell me about. One of these individuals is named Mike. The other was named Kehinde."

"I forgot all about them," I said, "Those two...Man, I can't believe that I forgot all about them."

"It's good that we are bringing them up again then because from what I can see from this file, they had a powerful impact on you. This file will be a centerpiece in our defense. Like the last file, I want you to be as detailed as possible. Agreed?"

File # 4
Fight For the Future

Sometime during the summer of 2007, I had received a phone call from Bee while she was out of state. She was feeling sad while on a beach, thinking about all of the problems that she had back at home. She wanted to see me in person when she got back. I was still pretty upset about the situation as a whole, but I always wanted to see her. When she returned home, I walked over to her house, and we talked it out. I tried to forgive her for what happened between us, but nothing that she said changed how I felt. I explained to her no matter what took place, I knew I was a good boyfriend. I tried to lay out my case to her, saying that what she said about me was pretty messed up and that she didn't have to go that far. She listened, trying to process what I was telling her, but I knew she wouldn't get it.

After speaking with her, I walked home while trying to relax my mind. The following morning, Bee called me once more. This time, the news she hit me me harder than when she told me she wanted to break up. She and her Mother were moving out of state in a month. I asked her why the hell didn't she tell me the day I had spoken to her before, but she didn't have an answer. I did not doubt in my mind that she would find someone else and forget about me. Bee was going to get with some guy, have some kids, while I was at home looking stupid, I told myself.

The month before she left were some of the hardest days that I had experienced in my life. I counted the days until she was going to leave. I was so conflicted. A part of me was glad that she was moving because if she did get with someone else, I wouldn't have to deal with it. The flip side of that coin was that I was losing a friend. With that in mind, I tried to see her as much as possible. We would see each other about four more times before she left. Her Mother asked me if I could assist them in packing up everything that they had in the house, which I reluctantly agreed to. When the day came for her departure, I hugged and kissed her on the cheek. I told her to write to me when she could. I went home, laid in my bed, and cried for about an hour.

Regardless of what she did, in my heart, she was my best friend. She was the closest thing I had to a real relationship, and she was about to go to some state that was on the other side of the country. Life went back to the way it was for me before I was with Bee. Summer school would begin soon, and I was not looking forward to it as I was still angry about everything. I stayed in my room, not doing much but playing video games.

One day, a gaming magazine that I subscribed to had an ad featuring a new Street Fighter game that was being released. It would be called "Street Fighter: Anniversary Collection." It was huge news because it would feature what's considered two of the best Street Fighter games ever created. One of those games was called "Street Fighter III 3rd Strike: Fight For the Future."

I had played this game when I was very young at an arcade called Sega City in Indianapolis. A friend of mine named George lived on the same street as I bought the game, and I would go over to his house to watch him play it. This Street Fighter was like any other before it because of how unique it was. It was Hip-Hop themed. The coolest part about it was as you were selecting your character, a rapper was spitting rhymes. I loved the game just because of that, combined with the tremendous urban style that it had. Once I had picked up a job at a shoe store, it was the first thing that I bought. I brought it home and fired up the Play-Station 2, and played until the late hours of the night.

One of the characters in the game was named Sean Matsuda. He was trained by one of the main characters of the series, an iconic character in the world of fighting games named Ken Masters. Sean was Brazilian, and he had this slick feel about him. I decided to play him to get a better understanding of the system of the game. After finally completing the arcade mode in the game, I thought that no one would beat me.

While playing one night, I remembered two of my friends who I used to enjoy the game with, Mike and Kehinde. They were older than me, but I had looked up to them due to how insightful they were. I could've used a little company then, so I decided to give Mike a call. He answered the phone with that cheerful voice that I remembered, which flipped my whole mood. I didn't even have to remind him of who I was. He was so happy to hear from me and asked me how I was doing. I told him that I needed some fresh air and wanted to know if he was down for hanging out. He said that he would be honored to have me over. I explained I had just picked up 3rd Strike, hoping to get back into Street Fighter again. He called me a "Rookie," which we both laughed about. He warned that he was going to get me back in fighting shape.

I told my Mother a few minutes later that I had talked to Mike again. I was going to hang out with him tomorrow if that was okay with her. My Mother was so thrilled that I was finally getting out of the house for once that she offered to drive me over. The next day, we drove out to Mike's apartment, which was surprisingly in walking distance. The apartment was right in front of a gas station in front of my high school. When we had arrived at the location, Mike and Kehinde were standing outside. They looked just like I had remembered them. Mike was about my height and had shaggy brown hair. He was wearing a white tee-shirt and blue jeans pants. Kehinde was a tall black man who had a smooth as hell dress style that made him stand out. They were the opposite of each other. While Mike was a fun-loving Street Fighter player, Kehinde was more reserved and relaxed.

I got out of the car and greeted them both with high fives. I told my Mother that I would be back later that night. The three of us walked into the apartment, and right away, I noticed the gamer vibe it had. There were two green sofas and a TV in the corner of the living room. Attached to the TV was a slim black PlayStation 2, with two arcade fighting sticks.

Once we got settled in, I began to talk to the two about some of the situations that I was dealing with. They were both very open to listening to my problems while giving me sound advice. They told me that I was one of them now so that I didn't have to worry about what happened in the past. Kehinde felt that I had a lot of potential, explaining that I should do what made me happy instead of worrying all the time. I don't think I smiled that much in a long time as I did during that talk. I had the feeling that I was home and that these two were my long lost brothers. They were so welcoming that I couldn't help opening up to them. After we were done talking, we sat down to play 3rd Strike. I was confident that I would be able to beat these two, but things...didn't go as planned. I took a fifty to zero ass-kicking that day, but I wasn't mad. It was just fun to talk trash (which I stopped doing after the tenth loss) and talk about Street Fighter.

We ordered a pizza then threw in an old school Kung Fu movie after. When it had got late, I told them that I had to return home and sign up for summer school the next day. They assured me that I was welcome anytime.

While heading back home, I felt that I had a place that I could go that would be less stressful than staying at home. I had new friends and a fun game to play. After I registered for summer school was completed, I ran back to Mike's apartment. The more time that I invested there, the more I learned. I got a chance to know more about both of my new mentors. I learned that Mike had two other siblings like me and had dealt with a lot during his childhood that was similar to my own. We were both loners, but we found refuge in gaming. He wasn't close to his father, as he wasn't really in his life but had a good relationship with his Mother.

Street Fighter was one of his biggest passions. It was his sport, and his goal was to become a well-known player. I didn't realize how big fighting games were before I had met Mike. I knew that there were tournaments, but I had little knowledge of some of the well-known players. He showed me a popular You-Tube video of two legendary players named Daigo Umehara and Justin Wong playing 3rd Strike. The two were very accomplished players that had a match at a tournament known as Evolution Championship Series. Evolution (also known for EVO) is the most recognized tournament in the fighting game community. The game between the two took place in 2004. In the video, Daigo, a Japanese player, was using Ken and Justin, an American player, was using Chun Li.

What made the clip so legendary was the one particular occurrence that took place. Justin Wong was dominating Daigo in that specific round to the point where his character Ken, couldn't withstand a single hit or else he would lose. Knowing this, Justin preformed a "Super Move" with Chun Li. In Street Fighter, there are moves known as Special moves that do what is called "chip damage." If your character blocks these moves, they will take less damage than they usually would if they were hit. Super moves also carried this property.

Daigo's character had one hit point left, so Justin did Chun Li's super move hoping that it would hit Daigo, and he'd take the victory. Daigo would then do something that no one expected. In 3rd Strike, there is a game mechanic called "parry." If a player taps forward on his control stick at the same time an attack hits him, the character being attacked will perform a parry, which gives them enough time to counterattack. Chun Li's super is one of the hardest to parry in the game, and it seemed like Justin's victory was assured. Still, Daigo had parried every single hit, then countered stealing the win from Justin.

The crowd went crazy. I had never seen someone do anything like that before. I didn't even know that Street Fighter could be played at that level. It made me realize that if I wanted to improve as a player, I needed to sit down and for once try to be good. I ran to my friend Poley's house to show him what I had just seen. He was so amazed by the video that he agreed to become my training partner. In no time, Poley had gotten better until there was a period when I couldn't beat him. He would wait for me to do something risky, then counterattack me. After getting badly embarrassed by Poley one session in front of Mike, Mike decided that he would make me a better player. He handed me a strategy guide that contained everything that I needed to know about the game.

His theory was that if I sat down and read more about the game, I may get a clearer understanding. So, I did. I sat on the sofa once Mike went to bed and read all night. I was so intrigued by what I was reading that sleeping was not an option. There was so much depth to Street Fighter than just mashing buttons. Each character had a set of hit points. All characters had different play styles that you needed to understand to be effective in a fight. Spacing your attacks and making sure that they hit at the right range was substantial. I learned about frame data, and while I didn't understand it at the time, I figured out that it determined pretty much every movement that your character made. The book explained how to perform super moves, along with which ones were the most potent.

Mike woke up and found me reading the book where he left me in the morning. He started laughing at me then asked me if I wanted to play some more. It was the perfect opportunity to test what I had learned. I skipped my regular morning routine because I had one thing on my mind that day. The moment the first round began, the difference was night and day. My movements were much smoother. I understood what I was looking at while I played. Mike was impressed that it took only one night for me to understand things so fast. I was even able to go toe to toe with Kehinde once he returned home and hold my own.

That feeling that I had once I was able to score a win was so gravitating. It was as if I stepped out of a war. Training rewarded you in the game. You could see the results on the screen. It reminded me of all the work that I put in when I still played basketball. When I stopped playing the sport, it left a void that I wasn't able to fill with anything else. That had changed as Street Fighter rekindled my love for competition. I loved something again. It was funny that a video game about martial arts could make me feel this way. It was therapeutic. Slowly but surely, the quilt that I carried for running away from basketball started to vanish.

Sean, the character that I chose to learn, was the weakest character in the game, but each character carried a sort of "message" behind who they were. I didn't know Sean was the weakest, but one of his personality traits in the lore was that he would never give up.

Once he had taken a beating (one of many), he would get back up, train and try again. There was no way to make Sean a better character in the game since you can't alter a character's design in a fighting game. There was only so far you go with a lousy fighting game character, but I saw so much of myself in Sean. He was trying to reach his full potential. No matter how bad a loss he took, he still tried to take on his world's most significant challenges. With that in mind, I kept playing him. I'd try and try again until I was ready to face greater challenges.

I continued going over Mike's and attending summer school.

I felt that I was stepping into a better state of mind the more time I spent with Mike and Kehinde, but I couldn't shake off Bee's thought. She would call me to check up sometimes, and we would talk about some of the past. My confidence was still a little shook. I spoke to my friends about it whenever I was feeling down, but it did little good. I would be happy one moment, then completely down the next. On a sunny afternoon at Mike's house, Kehinde came into the house and asked us if we would go dancing with him.

"Dance?" I asked them, puzzled at the notion, "Since when the hell do we dance?"

Mike told me that he and Kehinde had learned how to breakdance. For the last three years, they have been B-Boys. I knew how to dance, but I wasn't confident about it.

"If you are going to hang with us, then you are going to have to keep up with the crew," Kehinde said.

"Yeah, you are apart of the squad now, Jay," Mike said, "You comin'?"

At first, I was going to decline. I didn't want to be put in another position where I could be embarrassed. What if the people there ask me to dance? What if someone laughs at me? I realized that I was falling back into that same mindset that held me back for so long.

"Why not go?" I asked myself. "Why not go out and met some new people? Just go and try."

"I'll go, man," I said, standing up, "May have to show you guys how to get down."

"Right on," Kehinde said, "I'll see you there."

Mike and I waited for another one of his friends to come over. He was an Asian man around Mike's age. He was a nice guy like Mike, and he was also a gamer. The two of us got along quite quickly. On the way to the dance, I spoke to him about some of the games that I was playing at the time. We had a lot in common, which was becoming normal with many people that I had met through Mike. Once we had arrived at our destination, I was surprised that we were at the University of Illinois. We then walked a few blocks to a large building. There was a concrete open space where I saw a DJ playing these amazing Hip-Hop tracks. These weren't any of the records that I heard on the radio at the time. They were so much more heartfelt, each having an old-school feeling to them. The flow of the music drew you in by how chill it was. It was very similar to how 3rd Strike's music sounded.

I sat down on a nearby bench and just watched. Mike and Justin performed moves that I had no clue they could do. I had seen breakdancing before, but I never give it much thought. I was watching how much fun they had, though, it inspired me. I waited for about an hour, bobbing my head to the music. When they were done, I ran up to Mike, asking him to teach me everything he just did.

"Wait? Really?" he asked.

"Hell yeah," I said, "That shit was dope!"

He laughed then took me under his wing.

Dancing, though? I thought.

I couldn't believe that I was doing it, but it was a testament to how I was changing.

A day or two later, I began training with Mike and Kehinde. First, they made me watch a few DVD's called "Battle of the Year." These were B-Boy battles that took place in Germany. Battle of the Year was pretty much like the Breakdancing Championships and damn, could these guys dance. In all honesty, some of the shit that they did, I didn't think was humanly possible. I watched as many of the matches I could to learn the necessary steps.

Once I had seen enough, Mike decided that I was ready to start training. For about a week, I learned the necessary steps to breakdancing. I caught on to some of the basic footwork of which one of them was called the "Top Rock." For about two weeks, I would practice with Mike in his living room. When he thought that I was good enough, we returned to the University of Illinois. There was a larger group of people that were there this time.

In the past, that would have made me super nervous, but this time, it didn't. I was calm and ready to show off what I had learned. Once the music started, I jumped in the middle of the group and started dancing. The amount of fun that I was having was so genuine. I'd stepped out of who I was before that day and transitioned into someone else. It was equivalent to being reborn. I laughed and danced with Mike, Kehinde, and others that I had met. At one moment, while I was dancing, the group of people that I was dancing with all surrounded me and started to clap. Mike was the most excited to see this as he started yelling out moves for me to do.

"Do the six-step!"

"Show them your Top Rock!"

My body just responded to everything that he yelled, even if I couldn't perform a particular move very well. After I was done, the crowd broke out in cheers. They patted me on the back and gave me high fives. For the first time, I felt a natural body high. Kehinde came up to me, telling me that Mike had trained a great student. After telling me how excellent my performance was, he told me something that I would never forget.

"It's cool to be Justin McMullen."

When those words hit my ears, something in me just snapped. It was almost as if a button had been pressed somewhere within me. It wiped away out of all the negative things that happened to me. I never thought that it was cool to be myself. Hell, I never once considered myself as cool at all, but I knew that time was over after he said that. I could be a better human being than I was before. Happiness, drive, and self-respect, three things that I was sorely missing, became what I sought after. I sat down on the bench with a smile that went ear to ear. I didn't dance anymore that night after that. When I had gotten home, I laid down on my bed, reminiscing about the night that I just had.

It Was Cool to be Justin McMullen.

I began thinking about my life at that point. What Kehinde told me didn't feel like I gained validation; it was a reassurance. I asked myself an important question.

Why do you think you're a failure?

Any other time I would ask myself that question, I would say that I already failed. I failed in my relationship, school, and basketball. I was always running, but look at what happens when I put forth an effort. When I applied myself to something, good things happen. Nothing was written in stone just yet. I brainstormed about some of the qualities that I wanted to fix. I reminded myself that anything I would change was not for anyone else, I needed to do this for me. I tried to find strength. I wanted to dress better so I could see what I looked like when I tried to look my best. I pulled out my report cards and reviewed all my grades from the previous year. I needed fourteen more credits to graduate, which at the time, I had about seven. That meant that I had to pass every single class for the next two years.

I had to make sure that I did well in summer school to put myself in the best position to make it. That also meant that my study habits would need to improve substantially if I was going to pass. I had to get prepared for school. Sure, I had dug myself into a hole the first two years of school, but that didn't mean that I couldn't turn things around. I wrote down a list of things that I wanted to do then hung it up on my wall. It would be a day-by-day goal that I swore that would achieve.

After summer school classes the next day, I went over to Mike's apartment. I explained how I felt after what happened the previous day. He was thrilled that I, for one, decided to change and that he helped with that. Kehinde came home shortly after, and while we were playing, I told him that I wanted to take my life more seriously. As with Mike, he was delighted to hear this, saying that he didn't want me to turn out as some kid "that does nothing with his life." He asked me what my goals were, and I told him that the new plan was to complete high school for now. For the remainder of the summer, it was all about school first, Street Fighter second, and then dancing in my spare time. It was the perfect combination because I was always testing myself that summer. I was retraining my mind to focus on the things that mattered.

I re-channeled all of the energy that I gained from what people said about me over the years into something that fueled my drive. The key to success was figuring out how to appreciate who I was despite what I was told over the years. Taking small steps to get to the point was essential. When my junior year of high school had arrived, I was a different student. I began studying harder. I'd stay after school to use every resource that I had to make sure my grades were in the A to B range. Some of my classes were tough. God knows that I hated Biology and Math, but those were the only two classes that I struggled with in the past. English, however, was one of my strengths. I had the most fun in English, as I enjoyed being able to structure words and create stories.

Due to that love, I started writing storylines in my spare time.

I'd stay in the library at lunch instead of going out and read as much information as I could on how to properly structure a story. The information website Wikipedia was just taking off around that time, so I would use it to read about some of my favorite shows that I liked growing up. I started off trying to understand shows like Dragon Ball and Naruto, two very famous Japanese manga well known across the world. I studied more about

Akira Toriyama, wanting to know why gave the characters the names that he did and how he wrote his stories. Once finished, I turned my attention to my favorite movie, "The Matrix." The philosophies and the true meaning behind *The Matrix* gave me an appreciation for detailed storytelling.

With my mind always on literature, I got to the point where I would never go out to lunch. At some point that year, I had learned about the Anime club. It was a club where students that were fans of Anime could come together and watch popular shows. A friend of mine named An, a Korean student started the club. I joined soon and somehow became one of the leaders of the club. We would hold the anime club meetings every Thursday, with many students attending our meetings. I even got Poley to start coming to the club with me. I experienced a lot with the members that joined. They were just like me. Each one had gone through a lot as individuals and were just there to have a good time. Some of them I stayed away from in the past to protect my already damaged image. They were labeled "lames" but to be honest, they were some of the brightest people that you ever want to meet. Anime Club taught me that I shouldn't judge a person based on how they looked. Everyone had something to offer, not just those deemed popular.

Which brings me to a fellow student that I met named Aaron. Aaron was a softspoken person that I met while in Anime Club one day. He was down to earth. I explained to him that I was working on a story, and I showed him some of the work that I had created. He was an artist with a unique style. I had issues expressing my ideas because I couldn't draw to save my life.

He heard some of my thoughts, thought that I was worth the trouble, and agreed to draw my characters for me. Aaron was the opposite of me in almost every way. I had become driven and loud at that point at that time. At the same time, Aaron was calm and collected, never letting anything bother him.

I would always ask him, "Look, bro, why the hell doesn't anything get to you?"

He would shrug and explain that life was too short. This mindset of his helped me out quite a bit throughout that year. I had someone that I could talk to about gaming. We liked the same movies and stories. I would tell him about the crazy relationships that I had and asked him for advice. The best part about him was he never once in his life judged me. He never turned his back on me. I met his family, who were amazing people. Our friendship helped me continue to mature.

As I changed a lot about myself internally, I made serious changes to myself externally. The most significant issue that I had was my appearance. The money that I had gotten by working at a shoe store changed all of that. I made out a list of things that I like to wear. I would work extra hours on the weekend to ensure that I got everything that I wanted, never wanting to have to wait. My wardrobe issues came to a swift end. I went from two pairs of pants to fifteen, three shirts to twenty, and plenty of shoes. I had Jordans and Nike. I made sure that I bought a new outfit once every week while also assuring that I put money away to save. I created a foundation that made me a happier person. I'd finally regained control of my life. So much so, that college was something that I was taking into consideration.

The next two years went as planned. Then, before I knew it, I graduated from High School. I walked across the stage and received my diploma. The first thing I did was thank God that I had made it. I realized that it wasn't about the material things that I had bought or what anyone said about me. It was about what I carried within. My Grandmother used to tell me, "Whatever a man thinks in his heart is what he is." No amount of money or attention will ever change that.

Even with all that stuff that I had done for myself, I realized I didn't do it for validation. I never bragged about what I had to anyone. In the past, there was this goal that I was chasing to get everyone to like me or to get the prettiest girl I could. All I wanted to do was prove everyone wrong. Instead of chasing popularity like I felt I needed, I ended up becoming a better student. I found out that I loved to expand my knowledge and to write stories for people to enjoy. When I went to Chicago to visit a college for the first time, I knew what I was going to major in.

On the way back from the visit, I told my Mother all the things that I wanted to do.

"I'm going to graduate."

"I'm going to have a big family."

"I'm going to save my own life."

As in the title of Street Fighter 3rd Strike, it was a Fight for the Future.

Then What Happened

"That was the happiest I had ever been in my life. I miss those days. Sometimes I feel like the best days of my life were in those three years. I wish that I could relive certain parts of my childhood. My time with Bee before all that stuff happened with her, being fifteen again, roaming the streets with Poley."

"We all have things that we wish that we could relive, Mr. McMullen," Ms. Lawyer said, "You made a major change in your life during high school. You looked forward instead of backward, and you can do that again here. Right now. You can look forward to bettering your life again."

"My dad used to tell me that all that time," I said, smiling.

"Tell you what?" Ms. Lawyer asked.

"That I have to start changing my outlook."

"Then your Father, like you, is an intelligent man. You made an excellent choice to want to fix your life when you were at your lowest. I believe that you stopped running from the person you were scared of the most. Who do you think that is?" Ms. Lawyer asked.

"Me," I said. " I was running from myself. I was scared of my success just as much as I was my failure. It's the stupidest shit in the world to think like that, but I was so embarrassed to have eyes on me when I failed that even when I did something right, I didn't want to be seen. I did everything alone. I didn't want any comparison to anyone. I believed that if I ran away from my family, I wouldn't have to be measured up to my brothers. They wouldn't be around for anyone to say that they would choose them over me. I thought that my world would be better if they weren't there, and they never once did a thing to make me feel that way. I'm here in this prison, rotting away while people live their lives trying to do something with it. "

"No," Ms. Lawyer said, "You are not going to rot in this prison. You continue to exceed my expectations. As I said before, the first step of solving a problem is admitting that you have one. You don't have to run anymore. You made a stand once to face your demons. Pick yourself up and do it again."

"I want to," I said, " I do want to leave this place now. But..."

"Nigel," Ms. Lawyer said, " Nigel is preventing you."

"He thinks that he is saving me. He warns me that if I go back to my old life, the same things will happen repeatedly. I can't say that I disagree with him. Even after graduating, I fell back into the same damn mindset. There wasn't a happily ever after like I thought it would be."

"What do you want to do?" Ms. Lawyer asked.

"I'm afraid to leave here and go back home. Every time I see family, two sides always come out of me. One part of me feels as though I love them to death. On the other side, there is darkness. I remember everything that they said or how we all split up."

"You want your family back together after the divorce?" Ms. Lawyer said.

The question caught me off guard. I took a deep breath and shrugged.

"Yes. I want that so bad that sometimes I dream about it. The dream used to feel so real. I would be in my living room or somewhere in front of my house. You don't even realize that this happy moment that you are having is fake until you are about to wake up. I would be watching movies with my parents. They would be on the couch, and I would be with my brothers on the floor under our blankets watching old Disney flicks back at our old house again. Life was perfect. Then I would wake up only to realize that I was living in a reality that I didn't want to be in. When my early twenties arrived, nothing went as planned. No college degree. No great job. Nigel's warning was right. I went right back to who I was before."

"Life never goes as planned," Ms. Lawyer said, "But that does not mean that better days are going to stop coming. You love your family. You love your friends. It's very apparent that you want those moments back, but Mr. McMullen, they are gone. The best days are not behind you. You have been a prisoner to your past for so long that you stopped looking toward your future. Does it not terrify you that you have so much that you can look forward to in your life, but you rather be stuck not moving at all?"

"I don't know what to do," I said, wiping the tears stinging my eyes again before they began to hit my face, "When is the day going to come when I feel happy to wake up? How long is it going to take?"

"That is completely up to you. All you have to do is make a choice. Yes, it's easier said than done. It takes much strength to be able to make that decision. You have to get out of the victim mindset. You have to stop letting yourself be a prisoner to your past and start shaping your future. That's the only thing that matters right now."

"So, that's our defense, " I said. "We're going to tell the Judge that I'm going to work to change my future again like I did when I was seventeen?"

"Well, we have one more file to go that I want to go over. We have touched on that somewhat in our conversation just now. I believe it to be the key to getting you out of here," Ms. Lawyer said.

Ms. Lawyer stood up and collected files, putting them back into her suitcase.

"This is a great place to stop for the day," she said, "We made a ton of progress. We will pick up the momentum in our next meeting, and when it's all said and done will be able to make our case to the Judge."

"Do you think that we will have a chance of winning?" I asked Ms. Lawyer, "Like they said, I am a danger to myself."

"Honestly, we have a great chance of winning. There are a few kinks to iron out, but I have no doubt that you will not only walk out of here a free man but also a better person," Ms. Lawyer said.

She walked out of the interrogation room, patting me on the shoulder before she left. I sat in my chair, thinking about the lengthy session that we just had. My friend, Kehinde's words, kept echoing in my head.

"It was cool to be Justin McMullen."

What happened from then? Somewhere along the line, I had lost sight of that. Just as Ms. Lawyer had said, I was a prisoner to my past, and I allowed it to be blind me. I just couldn't let go before, but I recognize that if I was to ever get out of here, that I had to move on or else it would continue to have a hold on me.

"Justin," someone called out.

Peter walked up to me and tapped my shoulder, trying to get my attention.

"Come on, let's head back to your cell," he said.

I nodded in agreement.

We began to walk back to my cell. The possibility of making it out of here was obtainable. What if the crimes against me were the wake-up call I needed and I didn't know it?

"Hey, Peter," I said.

"Yes?"

"Why did you decide to stay in this prison this whole time?"

"I never thought you'd ask me a question like that, seein' how the only one you seem to talk to is Nigel. I'm happy that you finally asked me something," Peter chirped, "But getting to your question, I have to be here with you. I hate that it has to be in this way, being an officer who has to help guard you, but it's the way things are now."

"You don't seem to be much of a guard. Nigel seems more determined on keeping me in here than you,"

"Yeah, well...I guess I hate to see anyone be a prisoner. There are a lot of lost prisoners that I have had to guard. Some accept their sentence, thinking that they will never make it out. Others don't listen because they depend on listening to Nigel. They don't want to believe that the prison that they are in does them any harm. Ms. Lawyer and I share a passion for helping people our way."

"What's the history between you and Nigel anyway?"

"Without Nigel, I would be out of a job,"

I laughed, thinking that Peter was messing around with me.

"Out of a job?" I asked, "Nigel is the only guard that seems to like his job."

"It suits him. I can't deny the fact that he is better at his position than I am. We excel at two different things. He rather his prisoners remain in here 'safe and sound' as he likes to say. I instead show them that being behind bars in places like this solves nothing," Peter said.

"So, you have been to other prisons?"

"I have. Many across the world," He stated.

"Across the world?"

"It's a long story, Justin," Peter said. "It would take forever to tell you all of it. However, here, you are my priority."

"But why are you so damn happy all the time?" I asked.

"It's just a trait that I was born with that I like to share with others," Peter replied.

We reached my cell, and Peter took his keys and unlocked the cell door. I walked into the cell and sat on the edge of my bed.

"Ms. Lawyer informed me before she left that she would be in to see you at the same time in the morning," Peter said, "You should get some rest. You have a big day ahead of you."

"I will. Thank you," I said, lying down.

"See you tomorrow," Peter said, walking away.

I heard the steel door shut at the end of the hall. Could these be the last couple of days that I stayed in this cell?

"It's been seven years," I said, " It is time to be—"

"Freed?" a voice other than mine growled, causing me to look around my cell for its source.

Coming out of the shadows of one of the corners as if he were a ghost, Nigel approached me.

"I thought that we had this conversation before, Justin," he said, "My how far we have fallen."

"What are you talking about?" I asked, raising from my bed.

"I see that she has gotten through to you. You two had a delightful conversation today, didn't you?"

"She just wants to see me get out of here," I said.

"What do you want!?" Nigel yelled, taking a few steps closer to me. "You want to leave. You want to go back to that filthy, weak life that you had before! Don't you—"

"Yes, I remember everything, Nigel!" I yelled. "You don't have to keep reminding me anymore! I know what happened! I was there!"

"Who the hell do you think you're talking to!?" he snapped back, "After everything that I took you away from, you gonna turn your back on me?"

"I'm not turning my back on any—"

Enraged, Nigel punched me in my face, knocking me to the ground. Blood flowed from inside of my mouth down my jaw.

"You shut the hell up when I'm talking to you, little boy!" Nigel barked.

He pulled a crumpled piece of paper out of his pocket and tossed it at me. I grabbed it and opened it.

"I found that under your bed."

Hey Bro,

I have so much to tell you since I have been away. I have a lot of explaining to do—

It was the letter that I was writing to Cameron, but I tossed it away because I didn't want to give away too much information on the situation that I was going through here.

Oh no, I thought to myself.

"You didn't think that I was going to find out?" Nigel said, "This is my prison! I know everything that goes on in here."

I stood up, wiping the blood from my mouth.

"Sending letters back and forth to your older brother, huh? Stupid. Stupid. Stupid. From now on, I will never let you take a single step out of this cell. You have seen the lawyer for the last damn time."

"No," I said.

Nigel pulled out his nightstick and gave me a long stare-down.

"What the hell did you just say to me?" he said.

I spit the rest of the blood that I had in my mouth on the ground.

"I asked you a question, Prisoner," Holding a wide-eyed look, Nigel words were spoken slowly and deliberately as if to infer I was suddenly hard of hearing or dumb "What did you just say?"

"I said no," I repeated, matching his tone of phrase. "I will see Ms. Lawyer again."

A cold exaggerated laugh came from Nigel. He pointed his nightstick at me.

"Have you lost your mind?" he asked.

"I have let you control me for years. I can't do it anymore. There has to be something better than this, Nigel. I'm tired of the hate. There's somethin' better out there, and I'm going to find it."

"You ain't going to find shit but the same thing you have always found. Now all a sudden you're motivated? You haven't kept motivation your whole damn life. You are going to do the same thing that you always have done. Run when things get difficult. This little spark of yours won't last more than a couple of weeks at best, and we both know that,"

"You don't want me to make it," I said. "You want me to be in here stuck with you doing nothing but living in fear. I don't need that fear anymore. I'm walking out of here, and this prison can go to hell."

Nigel hit me across the face with his nightstick, though this time, I didn't fall to the ground. The strike didn't hurt as much as his last ones did. Nigel stood there in shock that the blow he dealt didn't take me down. He swung at me once more, but I caught the stick with my left hand this time. Nigel tried to pull the stick away from me as hard as possible but couldn't do it. I wouldn't let him

"I'm getting out of here," I said, "Without you."

Verses

I remember the day that I met Nigel. In one of the basketball games that I was playing when I was on the seventh-grade
basketball, I was driving to the hoop, and I missed a layup. I was
called for traveling by the ref and for some reason, I heard this
laugh in the back of my head. After the coach took me out of the
game, I never played much after that. I sat down, and I looked
over at my parents. My Mother had a troubled look on her face.
My Father had a smile, but it was one of those smiles that had a
meaning behind it. It was almost if to say that "Oh, he's just nervous." After the game, when I was changing in the locker room,
the voice of the laugh that I heard spoke to me whenever I was
in a situation that put me at risk of embarrassment.

Don't do this.
Don't do that.
I'm trying to save you from failing.

For years this was the only voice that I had heard. It became
so dominant in my life that I forgot all about the other voice that
told me to try out for the team or study hard. When I stopped
listening to the voice that was trying to warn me to run away, a
lot began to change. However, that voice still spoke to me.

All it did was remind me of my failures and stop me from
doing things that I had never even attempted yet. I let this voice
rule over me for a long time. Soon this voice became the only
thing that I would listen to, and before I knew it, I submitted to
its warnings. That voice became my safe zone. Then it became

the only friend that I thought I had. When I turned 22 years old, the voice had fully affected every part of my personality. I thought the worst of everything. No matter what happened, I was not enough. I would have dreams that I was getting embarrassed. My fears would constantly speak to me.

I would dream that I was back in at my old middle school...

Or overhearing another family argument...
Or seeing Bee with another guy that wasn't me...
Or being surrounded by a group of people pointing at me...

"Stop it..."

Or seeing my brothers with wives and I was alone...
Or watching everyone else that I knew succeed and I didn't...
Or that I hearing that I was ugly...

"That's enough..."

Or that someone was talking about me behind my back...
Or that I would never be anything...
Or my Mother loved my brothers more than me...

"I said that's enough, goddamn it!"

Or that I would never find love again...

"That's not who I want to be anymore!"

Or that I would mess up again....
Or that I would run again...

"None of that is true..."

Or that I would lose again...

   "It's not true!"

Or that I'm nothing...
Or she would leave me again...

   "enough..."

Or that Dad would leave again...

   "Enough..."

Or that I would be poor...
Or that I was boring...

Or that my life meant nothing...

I ripped the nightstick out of Nigel's hand and threw it to the ground. Nigel then grabbed me by the throat then slammed me into the wall behind me. I grabbed his wrist, trying to free myself, but his grip was too firm.

"How about I make sure you stay here as a corpse then, you little bitch?" he yelled, tightening his grip.

My vision began to grow darker. I did everything I could to break the hold, pounding Nigel's wrist with my fist. He then lifted me off of my feet. The breath in my body was leaving me by the second.

"I can't break his grip..." my subconscious quickly surmised in the struggle.

Darkness built up in my eyesight. Nigel was about to end me. I was about to live my last few seconds doing what I have been doing over the previous seven years: being defeated.

...No. No, I wasn't. Not now.

I kneed Nigel in the face. The blow broke his submission instantly, and he back-peddled. Blood began to flow from his nose. I leaned against the wall, desperately trying to catch my breath.

"You piece of trash!" Nigel yelled, rushing right at me.

I balled my right hand into a fist. When Nigel got just close enough for me to reach him, I threw a left hook aiming for his nose. My fist crashed into his face. I threw another punch with my left hand that caused Nigel to stumble across the cell, and he fell to the floor, grunting in pain.

"You bastard!" he yelled.

I looked at both of my balled-up fists and back at Nigel. I

didn't know that I had that type of strength. I had never thought about going toe-to-toe with Nigel before.

I always thought that Nigel was stronger than me.

I didn't believe that he could be hurt, let alone me be the one to hurt him. Yet there he was, squirming on the floor. I balled both on my fist once more and took a fighting stance.

"You want to play games!? Me verse you, huh!?" Nigel said, taking his thumb to flick the blood off from his mouth.

"I don't want this anymore! It's over!" I yelled at him.

"I saved you! You were nothing! Nothing but a loser! An embarrassment!" Nigel yelled back as he got back to his feet.

"You didn't save me! You never wanted me to leave here! I'm done running!"

"Oh? Really! So you finally found your balls, huh? Ya done cryin'? Nah...we're not done yet! I'm not done yet!" Nigel yelled, running at me at full speed.

My body just responded on its own when Nigel dashed toward me. We clashed in the middle of the cell headfirst then clinched. I held on tightly to his arms and tried to push him toward the wall. He ripped his arms away from my grip, and he punched me on the right side of my face. He tried to throw a kick intending to smash my chest in. I caught his foot and tripped him, knocking him to the ground. I jumped on top of him then repeatedly punched him in the face as many times as I could. He grabbed one of my punches and threw me off of him toward the cell bars.

My back hit the bars, and a sharp pain shot up my back. As

I held my back in agony, Nigel got on his feet and picked me up by my shirt. He slammed my back into the cell bars repeatedly. I pushed his arms to the side breaking his grip and threw another flurry of punches. I was throwing blows so fast that it felt like I hit every part of his face. I threw on last right hook with everything last bit of strength I could gather. The blow landed square on Nigels' jaw, causing his body to bend to the side. He went limp as he hit the ground. He laid there, groaning in pain. I leaned over, putting my hands on my knees as I tried to catch my breath. My heart felt like it was about to explode. It was beating so fast. I closed my eyes and held on to my chest.

"You son of a bitch!"

I quickly open my eyes to see Nigel once again rushing me. He grabbed me by my throat and palmed the side of my face with his other hand. He slammed me onto the bed, pinning me there. Blood was gushing from Nigels' mouth, and it dripped down to my face.

"You idiot! You won't find happiness! There is no one out there for you! You will not go back! I will not go back! WE WILL NOT GO BACK!"

I grabbed Nigel by the shirt.

"Yes...I will..."

There was a sudden loud cracking sound. Nigel's eyes then rolled to the back of his head, then he fell on top of me unconsciously. I looked above me, and Peter was there with his nightstick in his hand.

"I knew I heard something," he said, "Never thought that I would have to hit anyone with this thing..."

JUSTIN RYAN

I pushed Nigel off of me and threw him against the wall. I then searched for the keys to my cell on his body, finding them attached to a brown chain on his hip. I grabbed the keys breaking the chain with pieces scattering all over the floor.

"These belong to me now," I said to Nigel, still trying to catch my breath.

I turned to Peter.

"You gotta problem with that?" I asked him.

Peter raised his hands in the air and shrugged.

"It's your prison now, man."

Soon

Hey Cameron,

Sorry that it has been a while since I have sent you a message. I wanted to tell you that I'm sorry that I have been away from you guys for such a long time. There is a lot that happened since that day, and I'm sure that you are confused, boss. Well, Dad and I got into an argument, and then it just snowballed from there. I needed to get away, man. Just for a while to get stuff figured out. I don't hate you, and I don't hate anyone in the family. I feel like a bad brother for never coming to you with these things. I feel like a terrible person who never took the time to talk to anyone about some of the things that were bothering me for so long. Don't worry about it. I will be home soon, and we will catch up. Once I finish dealing with things here, I promise I won't waste any time returning home. See ya, bro.

Hello Mom,

I know that you have been sending me letters, and I'm sorry that I have been ignoring them. I am fine. I'm just taking care of a few situations that I have going on right now. I apologize for the last conversation that we had. Cameron told me that you have a new business that is going on and that you want everyone to come home to make our lives better. While I appreciate you wanting to do that, I don't care about the money. I would rather sit down face-to-face and talk some stuff out. There is a lot that I want to say to you, and I hope that we can hear each other out. I'll talk to you later. I will be home soon.

Hey Jordan,

Congrats on the birth of your daughter. I cannot wait to meet her for the first time. I know that you have been reaching out to me. I'm sure that you know that I have been ignoring you like everyone else. I'm sorry about that. I will come back to see everyone soon. I have a lot to ask you. Well, I guess I can ask you a few questions in this letter. How is the father life? How did you come up with the name Alaia and what does the name mean? Either way, I like the name. I will be home soon. Take care.

Hey Dad,

Sorry that I have been away for such a long time. I had to find out who I was and believe me it wasn't easy. Lately, I have been thinking about some of the stuff that you use to tell me about growing up. That I should try to get a better mindset, and I have all this potential to do more with my life. You were right. I wish that I had developed this mindset earlier, but it's better now than 20 years down the line. I hope that everything is going well with you and that you are taking care of yourself. I'm going to try to go back to the gym soon and get my body back to where it should be. I will be home soon.

THE 4TH CHAPTER
A Shift in the Tide

"Hey, old buddy," Peter said, knocking on the cell door's bars with his nightstick, "Wake up, would you?"

Nigel slowly opened his eyes. He sat up while observing his surroundings. He rubbed the back of his head and noticed a bump that he received from the blow that knocked him out.

"What happened to me?"

"I wound up knocking you in the back of the head when you were attacking Justin. I had to stop it from getting out of hand," Peter answered Nigel as plainly and politely as possible.

Nigel stood up, but his legs wobbled like noodles as he tried to maintain his balance.

"Where the hell is the prisoner?"

"Well, the prisoner is in his cell. However, Justin is in the interrogation room finishing the details of his case," Peter arched a brow as a coy grin spread across his face.

"What do you mean the prisoner is in his cell?" Nigel said, stepping up to the cell door.

"We have a new prisoner in here now. It looks like the new warden decided that you would be a better fit for this cell. Welcome to your new home. I hope that you will enjoy your stay,"

"Peter, this is not a game! Let me out of here now!" Nigel yelled, grabbing the cell bars and rattling them as hard as he was able. Nigel suddenly looked down for the cell keys that were on his belt. But he couldn't find them.

"Don't bother," Peter said. "The keys are now with their true owner."

"Release me from this cell now!" Nigel yelled. "I have authority here! This place belongs to me! Not some incompetent piece of trash like you! Now go and get my keys back. NOW!"

"Sorry, no can do. Bosses orders," Peter said, shrugging.

"What the hell do you mean bosses—" Nigel paused. He touched the side of his face, feeling the bruise that covered it.

"Justin. Justin took the keys," Nigel said, "But how...?"

"What do you mean, how? Didn't you feel the side of your face?" Peter said.

"Shut up, damn you!" Nigel yelled.

"He finally put you in your place. I thought that he would do it a little later down the line. I'm glad that he came to his senses. Never thought that you would lose to him, did you? It looks like the tables have turned."

"Bring the prisoner to me..." Nigel demanded sharply.

"He doesn't listen to you anymore. It's about time that I try my hand at giving some advice from here on out. You've had your fun," Peter said.

Nigel, enraged, reached toward Peter, trying to grab him through the bars. Peter grabbed his hand swiftly and twisted Nigel's wrist, causing him to yell in pain.

"Look at you," Peter said, "I have watched for years as you infected millions. I have seen you corrupt the minds of so many people as you constantly tormented them with your words. It is hard to get past you, Nigel. I'll give you that. However, you lose some, and you win some. But you will not beat him."

Nigel began to laugh lowly to himself.

"You think that he will stay away from me after all this time? I'll tell you the same thing I told that lying hag. You know him just as well as I do. Once he realizes that what is waiting for him, he will come back crawling. You watch and see, fool," he said.

"We will just have to see about that now won't we?" Peter said, releasing Nigels' arm.

Peter began to walk down the hall. He came to a sudden stop before he opened the gate.

"I wanted to thank you, Nigel. You have been a great help ever since we have been assigned to this place. Without a doubt, you have been the one that made all this possible."

"Don't get smug with me like you were ever clever enough to have planned all of this out," Nigel groaned as he sat down.

"I wouldn't go that far. Sooner or later, I knew that he'd get tired of your bickering. He might have a chance to walk outta here and live to tell about it,"

"He isn't out yet," Nigel said. "He may have gotten past me for the moment. The seeds that I have planted will bear fruit soon."

"Bear fruit, will it?" Peter said, turning around and walking back to Nigel's cell.

"This is over. He will open his eyes, and you will watch him leave. Then I'm going to do everything in my power to you make sure that your voice is so low that it won't have the smallest shot of being heard again."

With that, Peter turned his back from Nigel's cell to leave. But as he walked away, Nigel's reply crept into Peters's ear in a near whisper, causing him to stop, his words ringing as if Nigel was right next to him.

"That's the thing about me...you know that's all it takes... one lowly thought. And the collapse begins again. We can have a nice little chat when it hits him again."

Peter could feel his eyes snapped in his direction, but he didn't bother to turn around.

Darkest Before Dawn

I sat down in the interrogation room, waiting for Peter to walk in at any moment with Ms. Lawyer. The fight that went down with Nigel happened so fast that I didn't have time to think about it until I sat down. I looked at the keys to my cell that were lying on the table. I never thought that I would ever have them, let alone take them from Nigel, but now I have them. Now that I have them, what would I do with them?

"Yeah, exciting, right?" Peter said.

Peter was leaning against the wall with his hands in his pockets. I never heard him come in.

"Damn, I hate it when you and Nigel appear out of nowhere. It's like you are trying to give me a heart attack. What did you say just now?" I said.

"I said that it's exciting to be finally thinking on your own again. I remember when you were in high school in your junior year when you started to do that. I watched you put in hours of homework time and all that studying you use to do. It was a comeback worthy of a Rocky movie," Peter said, walking to the other end of the table and sitting down.

"Kind of an exaggeration if you ask me."

"Ah, you don't give yourself enough credit," Peter said. "You always were good at surviving to fight another day. Just ask your new sparring partner in your cell. Alternatively, you can look at the state of his face, whichever floats your boat."

I laughed. Peter always had a lot of jokes in his pocket to steal a laugh out of me before I got here.

"Now that I have you in a good mood enough to start a normal conversation again, I got a question," Peter said. "What made you fight him?"

"I felt I had to," I said. "I just reacted. Something just snapped. Damn, I don't even remember most of the fight. Only the end, when I was pinned on the bed. The way he was staring at me. All I could think about was trying to get up and get the hell away from him. It was worse than being in a cell all that time. It was almost like he was the cell itself."

"Good ol' Nigel," Peter said. "Guess he just bit off more than he could chew. I'm not shocked."

"Why aren't you shocked?" I said. "We haven't had many talks. I blow you off before you even get the words out your mouth. Didn't that ever bother you after seven years?"

Peter gave off a grin then shrugged.

"Of course it did, but that's not the bigger picture here, Jay," he said. "The big picture is that you snapped out of it before it was too late."

"You haven't changed at all, have you?" I said to him.

"Can't. It's how I was made. Good thoughts have to come from somewhere," Peter said, extended his hand out, trying to give me a fist bump.

I extended mine and met him halfway with our fists meeting in the middle. He sat back and gave me another smile.

"Glad the Nigel phase is over. Don't want to see you go back to that guy. Does a hell of a job at his job."

"Ain't lying about that," I said. "What's the word on Ms. Lawyer?"

"She should be here shortly. Don't worry about it," Peter said, "But I have one more question before she gets here."

"The sooner, the better," I said.

"Nigel said something to me before I came back here. He said that when you go back home and find out what's there, you will come back for him. He is pretty confident that you would at some point. Anything reason why?" Peter asked.

I bit the bottom of my lip. I rubbed through my hair and sat back in my chair. Peter knew the answer to that question already. There was one thing that I had left to face, and it was a weapon that Nigel would always use against me.

"Jay, listen," Peter said. "I understand that it still bothers you, but you have to deal with this thing before you get out of here. Every family has its problems. No one is perfect, but this has gone on long enough."

"What do I do?" I asked. "Everything that I thought I knew as a kid has completely changed."

"But that doesn't mean that you have to hold it in forever," Peter said. "You say that you want to face that darkness, well here it is. No more holding back. After I saw what you did to Nigel, I think ya got more than a chance."

"That fight made your day, didn't it?" I asked with a big smile.

"Yeah, I'd say so," he said, prompting a wide grin of his own, "Your lawyer should be here, I'll go get her. Be right back."

The Black File

"Hello, Mr. McMullen," Ms. Lawyer said, sitting down at the table and putting her suitcase on the floor. "You look—"

Ms. Lawyer jumped when she saw the bruises on my face.

"—Jesus! What happened to you?" she yelled.

I pointed to the keys on the table. She grabbed them and looked back at me.

" Are these the keys to your cell?" she asked.

" Nigel and I had a productive talk," I smirked. "In which he was nice enough to let me borrow the keys for a little while with some persuasion."

Ms. Lawyer sat in silence for about a half minute. She suddenly busted out with a loud laugh and clapped her hands a few times. Once she was done, she took a moment to catch her breath and then regained her composure as if nothing had happened. I sat there, dumbfounded by her reaction. Never once have I heard her laugh, but the news seemed so satisfying to her, that I just let her have her moment until she finished.

"Are you okay now?" I asked.

"Yes, I am now. Whew. Okay then. Now that I am here, I would like to go over the final file with you," she said. "We have gone over four files, Mr. McMullen. All of which has given me insight into why you were imprisoned here. How do you feel about your chances now?"

"I'm ready to get the hell outta here and go home."

"Wow," Ms. Lawyer said. "You have no clue how happy it makes me hear you say that, sir. I see whatever conversation you had with Officer Nigel ignited a fire in you of some kind. Must have been very constructive."

"You can say that," I smiled.

"So tell me what your analysis of everything that we have discussed so far?" Ms. Lawyer said, pulling out a black folder.

"I believe that after looking back, I understand how I got in here. It was a combination of a lot of different factors. I guess you can call them self-inflicted crimes. After something happened, I didn't know how to handle many things at the time. I was emotional and didn't have it in me put up a fight. So I stumbled. I stumble again and again. Now I realize in order to have a future, I have to make peace with the past. It's nothing to be ashamed of anymore. Now, I'm ready to stand in front of the Judge and prove my innocence."

"Excellent," Ms. Lawyer said. "Very good. However, there is one more file that we have to go over. It's the folder that I saved for last. If I may be honest, Mr. McMullen, it is one that I hoped we would be able to tackle once we got past the other files. Do you know what I'm talking about?"

"The break up of my family. The biggest reason I'm in here," I said.

"Yes," Ms. Lawyer stated simply, "That is correct, though this goes much deeper than that. When your family broke apart, I can tell that it left you bitter. Some of the details that I read informed me that you were once a very happy child before you went to Franklin Middle School. Going to Franklin indeed made you question who you were, but it was also the foundations that you were raised on that were broken. There is a reason why I saved this for last, one that I hope that you can figure out as we review this. Are you ready to begin?

"I knew that somewhere along the lines that I would have to deal with this," I said, putting my forehead on edge on the table "I wasn't ready for a long time. It's been a dry spot on my life for a very long time. I told you this before, but I would do anything to have those days back. Just like you said, they are not coming back. I'm ready to start."

"Now you're getting it," Ms. Lawyer said. "Let's go into the heart of the storm."

File # 5
Shattered Pillars

On September 22nd, 1989, an American network called ABC launched a programming block that would broadcast every Friday until September 8th, 2000. The block was titled TGIF, which stood for "Thank God (or Goodness) it's Friday." One of its most popular sitcoms was called "Family Matters." The series focused on Carl Winslow, a police officer and his family who resided in Chicago. Carl was married to a woman named Harriette, and together, they had three children: Eddie, Laura, and Judy.

At some point in the series, Carl allowed his sister Rachel and Mother Estelle to move into his home. The show was also known for its iconic character Steve Urkel, a complete and utter nerd who had a crush on Laura. Throughout an episode, the family would go through a trial of some sort. Whether it was an issue with the children or a problem that Carl was having on the police force, the episode would always end with a heartwarming resolution.

Carl or his wife would speak to one of the children and give them the guidance needed to become a better person. I would watch the show with my family every Friday. It became my idea of what a family should be. I believed that no family should ever be apart at the end of the day and that we should work through our issues no matter what happened.

Growing up, I had a good foundation. I had both of my parents in my life, and we were all fun-loving people. This trait came from my Father Jonathan, who would be just entering his twenties when I was born. He had a great love for video games, and he was the one that introduced me to Street Fighter. The weekends were terrific, as it was always something to look forward to. My cousins from my fathers' sister, Felicia, would always come over to visit us. We would tell each other stories, joke about television shows, and get into trouble every once. When Christmas would come around, everyone would come over our house to open our gifts together.

Since most of my parents' siblings lived near each other, there was rarely an instance where we didn't see each other for long periods. My dads' Mother, Nola, at some point moved in when I was around eight or nine. My Mom's parents, Doris and Edward, lived just a few blocks away down the street. My grandparents were crazy about their grandchildren. They did what they could to make sure that they helped raise my brothers and me to be good people. One of the foundations that they installed in us was having faith in God. We were a Christian family. Ministry ran through our family history.

Up until I was about eight years old, my uncle Charles Mc-Mullen was my pastor. He rented out a large church building where we would go to fellowship. He talked about the love of God and his son, Jesus. There were about twenty members that went to the church, all of which were my family. I remember the day my Father told me that he was going to be a pastor. I was so excited because my Dad would be talking about the glory of God to everyone. I was going to be a Pastor's son. On the first Sunday of our ministry, we drove to a large church located just across the street from my grandparents' house.

The building was called the Church of Nazarene. When we arrived there, a man named Tim and his wife greeted us. Tim was the head pastor of the church we were going to use. He was a very kind man and treated us like royalty. He gave us a tour of the church. I had never seen a anything like it. There was an area for kids with classrooms. There was a room for eating and a kitchen where we could go to make food. While it was very nice, it didn't compare to the beautiful sanctuary. The windows had pictures of Jesus with sheep. I had no clue that a church could have all of the options that it had.

When my Father gave his first sermon, he came out in a black robe that had a white cross on it. My Mother sat in the second row as always while she looked so proud to be the first lady. She would also be in charge of the children program that she had created herself. My brothers and I were the first members, followed by some neighbors that I knew. We would have substantial ministry anniversaries that would involve churches from around the country coming to visit us. I would watch people sing and tell beautiful stories about how God helped them come out of a trial in their life. We would also visit other fellowships, where my Father would be invited by other pastors to preach about God's word.

With the church being a large part of my life, it had a significant impact on who I was. I learned what it meant to give respect and love to other people. I did my best to honor what my parents taught me at all times. I was never in trouble of any kind. I made sure that I studied the Bible as much as I could because I wanted to be under God's protection. My Grandmother Doris would buy me cartoons based on the Bible to watch whenever I was with her at her house. She would give us assignments that came with the videos that tested us on what we had learned.

Due to our upbringing, we were quite different from the kids that we went to school with. I was seen as a little weird because I would try to talk to my classmates about God, sharing with them how he loved them when I was in elementary school. When I got in trouble or lied about something, my parents would discipline me. While it was either getting a "whooping" or being grounded for a month, my parents always made sure that I understood what I had done wrong. They explained that it was necessary so that I wouldn't do things that would get me into significant trouble.

That was their way to prevent that from happening, and it worked. This sense of family made me very loyal to the ones that I loved. I wanted to be the man that they raised me to be. I would make my parents proud. I wanted to grow up and continue to be close to my brothers.

As I got older, about in my early teenage years, this mindset would continue to develop and mature. I would always call upon God whenever something was bothering me, but soon, the very foundation that made me into the person that I was at one point was about to be torn apart.

Pastor Tim arrived at our house to visit one day while my Mother was cooking. I walked into the kitchen to see him standing there with my parents, who both had a sad expression. When I asked them what was wrong, they told me to go to my room for a little while. After Pastor Tim had left, my Dad said to me that Tim was moving out of town. It shocked me because Tim was always there for us. He had many people that loved him. Those people depended on him to guide them. We still needed him. Dad then assured me that everything was going to be okay, explaining that God told him that it was time for him to go somewhere else. At my age, this didn't make any lick of sense. Why would God ask him to do that?

About a week later, we were introduced to the new owners of the church. To be honest, I don't even remember their names. I remember the new pastor had red hair, and his wife always looked angry. Their son looked just like his Father, and he was about four or five at the time. For a while, everything seemed fine. They were kind enough to us. They even invited us to some of their plays they were doing. It seemed like we were getting along okay for the most part. However, something about the entire situation just felt off. I didn't get the same feeling of love that I had remembered from Pastor Tim. I couldn't quite put my finger on it, but I knew something was about to happen.

One year later, on a Sunday that I would never forget, we drove up to the church to begin ministry. Once we arrived at the church's front door, there was a letter taped to the window. The letter stated that we had busted a drum in the church, which we actually didn't do at all. Due to their ministry expanding, it also said that they didn't have any more room for us to be there. While my Father was reading the letter to us, my heart started to race. We walked back to the car in complete disbelief.

My entire family drove home in tears on the way back. Why would they kick us out? They wouldn't even speak to us. All they did was leave a letter on the door. If we were all children of God, would you stop us from coming to the church? Pastor Tim had a significant number of people come to the church at the time while still making time for us. He always made us feel welcome like he wanted us there. Now the people who said they "loved" us didn't have enough courage to tell us why we just lost our church home.

I don't recall going to church that much after that year. I tried to go to my Grandmother's church that she and my Grandfather ran in Danville, Illinois, but we didn't go every Sunday. Soon, we simply didn't go at all. Around that time, my Father became very invested in football due to the Quarterback, Michael Vick. Vick played for the Atlanta Falcons and was a fascinating player to watch. Dad would take us to a sports bar where we would go every Sunday to watch Vick play. There was a part of me that loved to go with my Dad, but I still missed our ministry. It felt weird that we didn't go to church like we used to. Eventually, I had grown used to it. I still prayed when I could, trying to maintain faith, but the feeling wasn't close to being what it once was.

As the years went by, I started to notice slight differences within our family. Slowly but surely, we began to change. When you grow up in a Christian family, especially being a child of a pastor, certain rules are established. We couldn't watch specific programs, we were not allowed to listen to certain types of music. We didn't curse. We didn't fight with one another, and if we did, we would typically forgive each other after. We weren't judgmental people by any means, but one of the things that we had was morals. If there was a situation that didn't look right, we were taught to avoid it. If there was a group of people causing trouble, we understood that we weren't better than them, but we did know not to participate in the activities they did. It was meant to keep our minds on being righteous people while staying away from "worldly things."

Those principles changed. All of the lessons that we were taught not to do became the norm in our lives. Not all at once, but they did change. As the years passed since our last sermon, my family continued to shift in a different direction. We were no longer listening to the gospel anymore. We were listening to rap music. There was cussing, and the vulgar lyrics touched on various subjects. I couldn't relate to anything that I heard at the time. What did I know about the streets? What did I know about popping bottles? What did I know about the "hoes"?

Not a damn thing.

I was a church boy. I didn't want to listen to any of that. I listened to music that was outside of the gospel before. There were the usual artists that anyone would know, but at the same time, there was a line that I thought was established on what was acceptable. It was a line that we wouldn't cross because then we would become the same thing that we preached against. I understood that it was just music to most, but I was taught that if you don't stand for something, you fall for anything. To add to the confusion, this was going at the same time that I was going to Franklin Middle School. I didn't understand the people around me anymore. Hell, I didn't understand the world around me anymore.

Music choice wasn't the only change. The way we spoke changed drastically. Like people who call themselves representatives of God, there is a certain quality that you are supposed to have. While growing up in church, I have seen people who act "holier than thou," when they're there. As soon as they step back out into the world, they might as well not even have come to church. They wouldn't do anything that they had preached or listened to.

The more the years went by, the more apparent it was to become the case with my family. All of us. When someone would say something out of line, we would all stare at that person, as if to say "I can't believe that he just said that." My parents would never argue in front of us in the past. When they did fight, it didn't seem like it was anything serious. Now, when they fought, it affected my brothers and me for days due to how intense it could get sometimes. I didn't know how to take it. I would start to shake whenever I thought that there was some argument going to happen. I became so good at telling when a fight was going to happen that it becomes almost like a sixth sense.

We were once a private family, but our issues became so bad within our household that the whole neighborhood knew about it. As for me, I became a walking double standard. I didn't get in any trouble growing up, but I still wanted to do some of the things that I saw my peers do because I thought they looked cool. Kids at my school got attention for doing the stuff my parents would kill me for doing.

Yet I held on to this idea that I was a "child of God". That I was going to hell if I disobeyed him. Whenever I went to hangouts or were with friends who liked to smoke or drink, that belief rang in my head. I didn't even enjoy going to certain places with my classmates because I knew that I was out of place. I can't tell you how many times I would sit at a get-together and not mentally be there. I tried to act tough to prove I could do it. I tried to drink even though I was not too fond of the taste of liquor.

I was split into two people, confused about who to be. Being a laughing stock at my school did not help this. I tried to talk about this with other people outside my immediate family. I wanted to see if anyone felt the same way that I did. But no one I reached out toward seemed to resonate with me like that at the time. When I tried to maintain the person that I was raised to be, I was told I was "sensitive". "You are so damn soft." One of my cousins went out of their way to tell me, "I ain't a real nigga."

So who the hell was I then? It was like being a small piece of a bigger puzzle only to realize that the designer had made a mistake on my piece. I would often ask myself, why didn't I go with the flow and change with them? Doubts started to sink in. I began to think that I was brainwashed. Maybe, everything that I was raised to believe in was a bald-faced lie. How could it not have been? If my family was willing to walk away from everything that we believed in, that meant it wasn't real, right? That question leaked its way into my soul.

God had left me.

He stopped caring because we turned our backs on him. I stopped praying and once told a pastor that wanted me to attend his ministry that I was done with "church shit." There was no reason to go back anymore. I told myself that I didn't care if my family broke apart because it was too late. It was already over.

We would reach our boiling point after I had graduated from High School. I came home from spending the weekend at Aarons's house. When we drove in front of my home, I found the back door was wide open. My Mother was standing outside with a troubled look on her face. I got out of the car and asked her what was wrong. She said, "Your father has left." I walked into the house and looked for him. I knew that he was gone, but I had to see it for my own eyes. He wasn't sitting in the same spot on the couch that he used to. All of the DVDs that he bought were taken. All of his clothes were gone.

And just like that, the family had ended.

All the talk about breaking up at some point finally became true. Everyone dealt with it his or her way. My Mother was genuinely saddened that he was gone. But my brothers and I knew that this was going to happen. Too much had taken place to think otherwise. I thought that one day, we would come back as a family and talk it out. Maybe there was a chance that we could come up with a reason to be together again.

That day never came.

With the divorce process completed, all of the members in my immediate family continued to go in separate directions. Despite a great deal of time passing, my brothers and I would still talk about what happened with our family. Everyone had their theory or knew something that they weren't willing to say out loud. I cannot speak for anyone else, but I can say that I never got over what happened. I was still angry on the inside. When I found out information that gave me more insight into what caused the divorce of my parents, it only made that fire within me worse, and my family felt the brunt of that. I rarely, if ever, agreed with the choices that they made. I would never approve of the women or men that they dated.

Every Sunday school lesson, sermon, prayer, and the foundation of my upbringing had been thrown out the window. When you look at your family as a child, they can do no wrong in your eyes. They are who you strive to be. When I was young, I looked up to them because, in my eyes, they were role models. Once you begin to grow up and develop your own logic, your view of the world becomes much clearer. People start to reveal who they really are to you. In doing so you learn that no one is perfect.

You want them to be perfect because you believe that they will never do anything to hurt you. I learned the hard way that no one is perfect. That even blood relatives can do you harm. I became a bitter person. My anger consumed me until the point where everything made me upset. I wasn't good at masking my feelings, and most of the time, I was an open book. I was never happy. I continued to look for other people to make me happy.

"I'm a good person. I deserve happiness."

"Why doesn't anything good happen to me?"

"Why do some people do bad things and get rewarded for it?"

No matter what I tried, the pain that I carried was still there.

Moving to another location didn't help because I was taking those feeling with me. Those close to me saw right through me. I would get heated when someone said something that I didn't like. When I dated someone, I came off needy, so they would never stay around long. The mindset that everyone is happy and had more than I had returned. I stopped caring about how I dressed when that was one of my chief complaints growing up. Sometimes, I would get so low that I wouldn't even clean myself properly because, at the time, I would tell myself that no one cared about me, so what was the point?

Money did not change the way I felt. When I was twenty-two years old, I got a job working at a call center. I got a small apartment and a car, wanting to restart my life once again. At first, the money was excellent. I was doing what I wanted to do. I was buying all the games that I wanted. I went where I wanted to go and made a lot of new friends. I had gotten back into playing Street Fighter hardcore once again. All of this seemed tremendous, but there was still something missing.

I went the next seven years with my life getting out of hand with rent and my bills. My job was extremely stressful. I witnessed people fall out of their chairs dead by the time they hit the ground. They were replaced soon after. As life started to become unbearable, a small miracle happened. I got called into my bosses' office one afternoon. When I walked in, three women were sitting down, one of which being my supervisor. When I asked what this was about, they told me that I had issues with attendance. I explained that I had not been late for six months, and as a result, my attendance record should have been cleared as a result of that. They denied my claim saying that I showed up for work three minutes late in December. That December in 2014 was one of the worst winters that we had in Illinois. The company that I was working for started to cut back on attendance policies due to how bad that winter season was.

I showed them a neighbor's video helping to dig out my car, but they didn't care. They wanted me gone and fired me right then and there. I handed them my badge and walked out of the building. While driving back to my apartment, I called my Father, explaining to him what had just happened. I was distraught, thinking about how I was going to pay my bills. He told me that I should try to dig deeper instead of working a regular job for the rest of my life. He asked me if I ever put any thought into going back to finish school.

I didn't get a chance to finish college when I left High School. I had to move back to Champaign due to financial reasons. Two years later, I moved back to Chicago with my Mother. I didn't think about school or writing, and when Dad brought about the idea of going back, I remembered that was a goal I wanted to accomplish. I told Dad that I would look into it. I went on the internet trying to find schools that had programs for creative writing when I came across a college called Full Sail University. Once I did enough research on the school, I decided to call them to see what steps I needed to take to enroll.

I spoke to an advisor who told me all of the great classes Full Sail had to offer. My excitement grew while talking to her. I stayed on the phone with her for about an hour to make sure all my questions were answered. I told her that I would like to join and gave her my information. When the call was over, I started jumping around in my living room. I had a new goal that I needed to achieve. I wasn't working for anyone's dream this time. I would be working on my own. I started pulling out my old stories that I used to write and rewrote a few of them to prepare myself for class. When my first day of school started, I went in with the mindset that it was all about me.

When it was all said and done, the next four years showed me what the anger I had within myself had done. I couldn't control my families' actions. I never dealt with divorce correctly. That was between my parents. That was a journey that they had to take. We were all hurt by it, but I needed to learn to let go and do all that I could to make my life what I wanted it to be. I cannot entirely agree with everything that they do. I get mad thinking about it because I know that a lot could be better. That rage would have followed me for the rest of my life. It was a darkness that clouded everything around me and caused me to miss out on so much.

It kept me from loving.

It kept people from wanting to be around me.

It kept me from seeing the birth of my niece.

It kept me from seeing my nephew grow up.

It kept me from making the most out of days.

It kept me from being in the moment.

It kept my mind focused on the past.

I'm happy that nothing happened to any of the people in my family while I was away. Tomorrow isn't promised to any-one, but I could make the best out of the time that was given to me. I could let that darkness go. I could find some light again. It didn't matter how things looked to other people as long as it seemed right to me. I needed to stand for what I believed in. I have that right. I have to tell myself that I was worthy of having good things in my life. It didn't have to be about pain and anger. Life was about more than that. I just needed to make a choice. There is always a choice. I just needed to remind myself that I had one to make.

Court Date

"Thank you, Mr. McMullen," Ms. Lawyer said, closing the file. "That concludes our preparation for the case."

"So, we are ready now?"

"Yeah, I think so," Ms. Lawyer said. "You have enough evidence here to show what put you in such a mental state. There is also enough to show that you don't belong in a prison cell. I am now a hundred percent sure that you can win the case now."

"I feel the same," I said. "I'm ready to go home. I have to make all of this right. So what's next?"

"The ball is now in your court, Justin," she said. "This is your prison, so now you have to decide the court date."

That was the first time that I ever heard her refer to me by my first name. She was always all business. There wasn't ever a time where she was not professional, but now even her voice sounded different.

"What are you talking about, Ms. Lawyer?" I asked. "How can I choose the court date? Isn't there a process to all this?"

"I want you to think back to something that you have told me while you were going over your last file," Ms. Lawyer said, standing up. "You said that you had a choice to make. You still do. This is your prison. You submitted to this place, so now you must decide when it's time to leave."

She grabbed her suitcase and walked toward the door.

"Wait!" I said, getting up and blocking the door. "You never told me who you were. Who are you? Why did you help me? How come I can't see your face?"

Ms. Lawyer took a deep breath and rubbed the side of my face with her hand. Her touch said a million words at once. It was a mothers' touch that I hadn't felt for a very long time. It was as if she said that everything was going to be okay without saying a single word.

"I want you to have this," she said, reaching into her pocket, pulling out a folded card in half. "This will tell you all you need to know about me. When the time is right to open it, you will know."

She opened the door and walked out. I stood in the doorway of the room, watching her walk to the entrance of the prison. Once she got there, the lights in the hallway began to illuminate brighter than before. Everything in prison was now visible. I could see the gray brick walls and the gray-colored floor. I could see the sunlight coming out of the windows. I looked down the hall to Ms. Lawyer, only to find that she was gone. I looked down at the card that she handed me and put it in my pocket.

The gate leading to my cell down the hallway opened slowly. Peter walked out into the hall as he stared at the light bulbs on the ceiling.

"Good. Justin broke through," he said.

Peter looked toward me and waved.

"This place looks completely different with the lights on, doesn't it?"

"It's still hell," I said, walking toward Peter. "Ms. Lawyer left a few seconds before you showed up."

"Yeah, I know. It's okay. It looks like my time as a correction-al officer is finished. Not a career that suits my taste, that's for sure," Peter said.

"You're quitting? You are just going to leave me here with Nigel?" I asked.

"This place no longer requires my service. I'll still be around when you need me. We have a lot to get done—some more trails to face. The journey doesn't stop here," Peter said, taking off his badge and throwing it down the hall.

I asked him, "Where can I find you when I get out of here?"

Peter smiled and patted me on the shoulder.

"Believe me. You won't have to look for me when you make it out of here," Peter said as he turned around and walked toward the prison entrance. "I'll be waiting for you after the court date. Don't take too long, my friend."

He opened the door then quickly turned around.

"Oh yeah! One more thing! I've meant to ask you this for some time. When I told you about Ms. Lawyer coming to speak to you about your case, why did you agree to it?" Peter said.

"What do you mean?" I asked.

"You were so quick to deny any help. You didn't read your letters for years. I was sure that you were going to tell me to leave you the hell alone or something along those lines. What made you decide to talk to her?"

"Nigel had me convinced me over time that this place was a haven. For a while, I thought that it was too. However, when you told me that someone had come to try and free me, I needed to find out if this place was what I thought it was, or if I was just running again."

"I get it. For what it's worth, I'm glad that you tried," Peter said.

"Thanks. Thank you for everything," I said.

Peter then gave me a salute and closed the door behind him. I took a deep breath and walked to my old cell. As I walked down the hall, I could hear Nigel humming. When I reached the front of the cell, he stopped.

"So, the lawyer plan worked after all?" Nigel sat on the floor, his face still bruised.

I sat down outside the cell bars, facing Nigel.

"Yea, it's over. I'm leaving as soon as I can," I said.

Nigel gave a soft laugh, then starting coughing.

"You...you've done something like this before, remember? What makes you think this will have a different result?"

"I remember a time that I was in a basketball camp. Our coach made us say a whole bunch of motivational lines and whatnot. I thought it was stupid as hell for the longest time, thinking that it had nothing to do with playin' ball at all. You should remember that. They made us memorize them, and then we would have to say it in front of the entire camp. There was always one that stood out to me. For the life of me, I didn't know why, but now I get why it did," I said.

"Yeah? What the hell was that" Nigel growled.

"If it's to be, it's up to me,"

"Pff...slap that on a shirt and sell it why don't ya." Nigel scoffed, laughing some more. "You going to bore me to death with some trash that you were told, knowing you are just going to throw it away once some more stuff goes wrong when you're out there? Spare me the 'I'm a different person now' speech. I've heard it. I've seen it. A million times before."

I shook my head.

"Thanks," I said.

"For what?"

"I've been listening to you for so long. I've always taken what you said as gospel. I thought I was safe. Now that I think about it, I always thought of it in just one way. You showed me that I wasn't living. If I continued to stay in here, I would've shut my eyes for the final time, never knowing what could happen," I said.

"The same thing's waiting out there for you. You can't get over it. You will never get past what you are. When it's all said and done, the people that hurt you the most will hand you right back to me. You won't admit it. But I was right. You are still just a little fool—just a glutton for punishment waiting for a badge of honor that will never come. For all of your altruism, your good intentions, there is no happy ending for you. You'll see...with open eyes,"

"Nah. I know I can't control anyone, or what anyone does but I can sure as hell I can control what I choices I make, " I said as I stood up.

I opened the cell door with the keys that I had taken and walked in.

"Leave. And don't ever show your face to me again," I said.

"Sure thing, boss...just give me a ring when you come to your senses. You know where to find me..."

Nigel began to fade away slowly second by second while staring at me with his red hate-filled eyes. His badge that he wore so proudly hit the ground once he was ultimately out of my vision. Nigel was gone for now. I had won this round. I knew that he could return if I allowed him to, but then more than ever, I had to leave. It would be a hollow victory if I didn't. Ms. Lawyer told me that the court date would depend on me because this was my prison. The time to leave had come.

THE FINAL CHAPTER
Judge, Jury, and Sentence

For the next few days, I sat in my cell alone. It was quiet in here. I couldn't believe that actual sun rays were coming in through the windows. I could hear the wind outside that I couldn't before. I looked out of the window, dying to see what was out there. I saw a cliff and beyond the cliff was the ocean. It was vast, endless, and beautiful. I wanted to go out there to jump in myself. I couldn't swim for the life of me, but it felt like the ocean was calling to me. I just needed to get out of this place.

The Court Date.

I had enough to state my case to the Judge. There was no way that I could lose. I walked around my cell, thinking about the court date and what I was going to say to the Judge.

"Look, Your Honor. I'm innocent. I'm no longer a danger to my self. You've made a mistake."

That opening sounds dope. I could say something along those lines. I'll walk in the courtroom like I own it. Ms. Lawyer would know how to follow up. I started pacing in my cell from wall to wall. Why can't the court date be today? I hope that she returns soon, man, so I can tell her to get this over with.

"Man, I'm bored," I told myself. "That should be one of my

first goals when I get out of here. Never be bored again. I want to spend days having more fun. Go on more vacations. I'm doing that every year from here on out. Hong Kong, Brazil, Tokyo. I want to go everywhere."

I started doing small things to pass the time. I would shadowbox in the hallway. I tried doing the Top Rock dance move I learned from Mike. Anything that I could do to make time move quicker. I sat on my bed and took a deep breath.

" What the hell do you mean I decide the court date? How does a prisoner choose that? How could one man have all that power? And now I'm quoting Kanye songs. Damn. Wow. Okay, there has to be something that I'm not thinking about."

I went over the five files in my head again. They all took place in a specific period. My crimes were called self- inflicted.

Self-inflicted...

There was something about that phase. I inflicted these crimes on myself. I helped build this prison.

I looked at my surroundings once more.

"God, this place is so ugly. How the hell did I let myself spend seven years in this dump? I want to tear this crap down."

I heard an object hit the ground in front of me. I looked down at the floor to see a grey brick shattered into pieces.

"How the heck did that happen?"

I stood up and picked up a piece of the brick that just fell. I looked above me at the ceiling and noticed that there was a square sized hole missing.

"This fell from there? This place falling apart now?"

I threw the piece that I had in my hand to the floor. That

was the first time that I had seen that happen before. Granted, it was always so dark in this place that I couldn't tell if it was still held together or not. I decided to take a closer look around the prison. I got off from my bed and walked down the hallway. This building was so dry. All of the walls are of brick and the floor of concrete. There were multiple small windows in the two halls, but looking outside of them felt more like torture than anything. Whenever I looked out, I was teased with freedom. I could still see the cliff and the blue ocean waves.

I walked into the interrogation room, where I would speak to Ms. Lawyer. I stood in the doorway for a few minutes, reminiscing.

"This is your prison, so now you have to decide the court date."

I walked back to the cell, still observing my surroundings as I went. I laid back on the bed once I got there and fell asleep. I woke up the next morning, still wondering about how I was going to see the Judge. I grew more and more frustrated as I spent more needless time here. Peter and Nigel were gone. There were no more meetings with Ms. Lawyer. I did everything that I was supposed to do. I got the help that I needed.

"Let me out of here!" I yelled at the top of my lungs.

The sound of loud crashes of stone rung through the cell as they hit the ground. The noise startled me. On the far right of the cell, more bricks had fallen from the ceiling. This was the same thing that happened yesterday. This place was falling apart. Somehow, someway, the prison was breaking apart. It didn't make sense. Is the prison trying to stop me from leaving?

Wait a second.

I yelled just now. I yelled that I wanted to get out of here. What I'm saying out loud was the key. Ms. Lawyer was trying to tell me something before she left. I paced back and forth in the cell.

"Okay, Okay. What are you trying to say to me? There is something that you what me to understand, but what is it? Damn it. Come on, Justin, think. You get to decide when you want to face the Judge. There has to be a clue. Why would you be the one to pick the date? Why me out of all people?"

I started hopping up and down on my toes.

"Come on. Come on. Come on. What are you trying to tell me, Ms. Lawyer? Why would I have control over the damn —"

I stopped hoping.

"I'm a prisoner to my prison. I don't have control because I'm still a prisoner here. I haven't taken full control just yet. That's what I have to do."

I started scratching the top of my head while I was thinking.

"What do I not have control of yet? Something is keeping me a prisoner here because I don't have control over it yet, but Nigel is gone. I beat him, and he left. There was no one else to face. Dang. What is it?"

Ms. Lawyer's five files that we went showed me how I lost control of my thinking over and over. Nigel had gained control of my thinking. It did more than keep me in a depressed state. They damn near imprisoned every part of --

"Oh, my God. That's it," I said. "This prison. Nigel, Peter, and Ms. Lawyer. That's what this is. I'm a prisoner of my mind. That's why I can't leave yet."

I understood then. It hit me like a ton of bricks. Ms. Lawyer wasn't talking about the court date. There never was a court date. There was just me. I had to stop being a prisoner to my mind. This prison was not a safe haven, but chains that prevented me from trying to change any aspect of who I was. I was not fighting a physical battle when I had fought Nigel. My anger so blinded me that I couldn't see what this place was doing to me. That's why I couldn't see Ms. Lawyers' face. It was the reason why she never told me her name. I was the source of the darkness in this place. Peter would try to help me by telling me that I didn't belong here, but I never listened to him. I was the one who needed to decide if I was going to fight to get past it.

If this was indeed my mind...

Then I can control it.

I was my judge.
I was the jury. I gave my sentence.

I balled my hands into a fist. I ran to the walls on the right side of me and punched it. The wall burst into rubble. I went into a fit of rage as I looked at the prison around me. I was going to destroy it piece by piece. I ran through the prison, punching and kicking as I went. Every punch that I threw added a sensation that I had never felt before. I could feel the wind come in from the outside.

I went into the integration room, picked up the chair, and used it like a baseball bat, slamming it into walls. I left the prison. I didn't just walk out of the front door. I tore down the limitations that I had set for myself. Tomorrow wouldn't just be another empty day. Now, I was looking forward to the gift of every sunrise.

The Lawyer and the Name I Could Finally Say

Taking a moment and breathing in the air for the first time in a while was the sweetest feeling that I'd had in several years. I looked up into the sky. It was blue and filled with full white clouds. The sound of the ocean waves drew me to the cliff. Once I got to the cliff, I stood there, gazing upon the endless ocean. It was powerful, vast, shapeless, full of potential. It could adapt to anything.

"That's more like it," I said with a huge smile.

After I was done basking in the brilliance of the world around me, I turned and noticed a dirt pathway leading down to the shore. I followed the path until I reach a beach. I walked into the sand, heading toward the waves that reached into the shore. The water was cold at first but got warmer as I stood in it. I crouched down, scooping up some water, and splashed it on my face.

"Whew," I exhaled. "Damn, I needed that."

I started laughing and sat on the beach for about an hour. I was free. The prison is behind me. There was no looking back now. Now, I had this vast, endless ocean in front of me, and with it came an infinite amount of possibilities. I stood up and brushed the sand from my pants. I continued to walk across the shore when I came across a small brown boat sitting on the beach.

"What? How did this get here?"

There was a white envelope lying on the seat on the boat next to two wooden paddles. I picked it up and opened it. Inside was a white piece of paper that had a message with a single sentence.

Just sending out a little positivity. —Peter

Peter. He was still looking out for me even now. I pushed the boat out into the ocean, got in, and began to row. After about two hour of rowing, I barely see the island that I had left. I didn't know where I was headed, but I knew that wherever I would end up, it was better than being chained up and not moving at all. Out of nowhere, a strong gust of wind blew toward me. The wind knocked me off on my back inside the boat.

"You gotta be kidding me," I said.

The sound of thunder cracked throughout the sky above me. The clouds started to turn grey with flashes of light going off inside of them. A storm was coming. Just when I had finally left my cell, more opposition had shown itself.

"No, not now," I said. " I just made it out."

While I stood up and brushed myself off, I felt something in my pocket. I reached in and pulled out a card folded in half. It was the last thing that Ms. Lawyer had given me before she left.

"Ms. Lawyer," I said. "I guess it's time."

I opened unfolded the card, and there was a single word on the card. It was her name. It was also the word that I was not ready to say when I first met Ms. Lawyer, but now, everything she had done for me became crystal clear. What she gave me was more than her name, but a word that I needed. It was a gift that she left. I placed the card on the inside of my shirt and carried the one word she passed to me into the storm.

Faith.